TALES OF WORDISHURE: BOOK I

BY
MICK MCART

Illustrations by:
Mick McArt
&
Mariah Anderson

MICK ART
PRODUCTIONS LLC
PUBLISHING
www.mickartproductions.com

To Caedie,
Welcome to
Wordishure
Mick McArt

Tales Of Wordishure: Book I
A Book Of Christian Children's Stories
All Rights Reserved
Copyright © 2013 Mick Art Productions
V2.0
Original printing (v1.0): 2009

Mick Art Productions, LLC
www.wordishure.com
ISBN: 978-0-9827000-0-6
Library of Congress: 2010934437

PRINTED IN THE UNITED STATES OF AMERICA

CONTENT

This book is dedicated to my Lord and Savior, Jesus Christ. Thank you for helping me find my way, giving me a new direction, and for writing my name in the Book of Life.

The Lord Jesus Christ is the heart of Wordishure.

A special thank you to my wife, Erica, who encouraged me to write this and helped me when I fell into times of doubt.

And to my son Micah, my gift from God. I hope we have many adventures together in Wordishure.

Thanks to my dad for my work ethic, and my mom for encouraging my artistic growth. Thanks to Pastor Scott McIntyre, for showing me that what I can do makes a difference. Thanks to my co-workers who helped, encouraged, and prayed for me as I wrote this book. I cannot thank you enough.

A special thank you to Mariah Anderson who helped me with the illustrations. You have helped bring Wordishure to life!

To the reader:
Thank you for entering the Land of Wordishure, I pray that this book will be fun for parent and child alike.

Visit the website and read the bonus story,
"The Button Doll of Wordishure"
www.wordishure.com

I would like to hear your opinion, contact me at:
E-Mail: mickmcart@gmail.com
Facebook and/or Twitter: Mick McArt

The Skipping Stone of Wordishure

"And Zacchaeus stood, and said unto the Lord: Behold, Lord, the half of my goods I give to the poor; and if I have taken any thing from any man by false accusation, I restore him fourfold."
Luke 19:8

Edward loved to skip stones. He could make one skip easily nine or ten times. One stone he had thrown skipped so much that he lost count! Today, he thought to himself, "I'm going to skip one across all of Lil' Valley Pond!"

Grandma had sent Edward out with a basket to collect squishberries, a delicacy in Trusthymn Village. But, after a few hours of picking berries, Edward decided to practice skipping a few stones. Not long after walking along the shore of the pond, Edward found the perfect skipping stone. It was smooth and round, like one of Grandma's squishberry pancakes! He paused for a moment and thought about saving it for the perfect day, but everyday is perfect in the land of Wordishure!

His sandals made a "schlop, schlop, schlop," sound as he waded out ankle deep into the pond. The water of Lil' Valley Pond was cool and refreshing. He loved it when his parents brought him here for picnics and swimming. He hoped to be baptized here when he was ready.

Edward waited patiently until the wind died down. Then, as the birds hushed their singing, and the sun was high in the sky, he slowly drew his arm behind his back. With a mighty hurl, he sent the stone flying. It flew straight down the center of the pond. Edward was pleased.

Knowing it would make it across the pond, he started counting the skips. The perfect stone skipped, tapped, spun around, and tapped again. Suddenly, there was a "tap, tap, a thunk..." and a big "ouch!"

"Tap, tap, thunk...ouch?" Edward thought. That doesn't seem right. There should have been more taps, maybe even a thunk, but never an ouch. As Edward pondered this sound, a mysterious voice from a nearby lily pad spoke to him, "Excuse me sir, is this your stone?"

Edward looked down and saw a frog with a large bump on its head. It was holding the perfect skipping stone that the boy had just thrown.

"I am sorry," said Edward sheepishly. "I did not see you out there."

"I don't usually see stars until nightfall," commented the frog, rubbing the bump on his head.

"My name is Edward," stated the boy, pocketing the stone the frog gave him. "I'm practicing to become the best stone skipper in Trusthymn Village. Who are you?"

"Hmmm...," said the frog. "I don't know, I don't remember what I was doing here."

"Why, you're a frog," insisted Edward.

"That would explain my weird craving for bugs," remarked the frog.

"Yuck," said Edward. "You should try squishberries, they're much better. I've got some in a basket right over here."

"Okay, but there's a swarm of delicious fat gnats over there with my name on it," the frog responded.

As soon as they reached the place on shore where the boy had left his basket of squishberries, Edward noticed that it was gone! "Oh no!" cried Edward, "I spent all morning picking squishberries for Grandma, and now they're missing!"

Edward was very upset. He knew Grandma had promised to make squishberry pancakes for all the people at church. Edward loved attending Fellowship Church every Sunday, and to be with others who loved Jesus.

Fellowship Church was a big ship that floated on

Waterdove Lake. Edward enjoyed holding his grandma's hand as they walked down the wooden dock leading up to it. Although the dock to the ship was narrow, it was also stable and sure. You'd never fall off as long as you kept your eyes looking forward. He knew some people that had fallen off, but they were watching their feet instead of trusting what was before them.

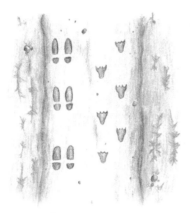

Every Sunday, Fellowship Church would float out on the lake with the sounds of joyful hymns, and the preaching of God's Word emanating from the heart of the vessel.

"Look," observed the frog. "A trail of squishberries! Whoever took them was in a hurry, and real sloppy!"

Soon Edward and the frog were walking and hopping down the trail of the missing squishberries. "You don't have to hop, Edward," said the frog.

"I like hopping," revealed Edward, bouncing up and down.

As they walked away from Lil' Valley Pond and through Whittlewood Forest they came to a clearing. "We're at the top of Tumbledown Hill," noted Edward, looking at the sign that named the location.

It was a tall hill with thick green grass that was much too tempting to resist. "What do we do now?" asked the frog.

"Just like the sign says, mister frog. Let's tumble down the hill," giggled Edward.

"Good," said the tired frog "because my legs are fried!"

Edward and the frog took a few steps down the hill, crouched down sideways and then began tumbling down the hill.

"This is fun!" shouted Edward.

"It sure beats walking," laughed the frog, "but it sure is making me dizzy. I can't remember ever being this dizzy."

"You lost your memory, remember?" Edward noted, tumbling along.

"Now I'm really confused," expressed the frog as they reached the bottom of the hill.

"Help!" exclaimed another voice.

Edward looked all around him and could not see anyone.

"I'm up here," came the voice from above his head.

Edward looked up, and there, fluttering over him, was a very worried-looking firefly.

"Help me, sir! There's a frog over there and he's looking real hungry," the firefly shouted, flying behind Edward to hide.

"Don't worry friend," reassured Edward. "He's helping me look for squishberries. He won't eat you."

"Fireflies give me heartburn," croaked the frog while tapping his chest. "That's something you never forget!"

"Did you say squishberries?" asked the firefly.

"A whole basket of them," pleaded Edward.

"Someone just came through here with a big ol' basket of them," revealed the firefly. "And they were in a big hurry!"

"Please help me find them," pleaded Edward. "It is really important."

"There is one catch," responded the firefly. "Mister...?"

"My name is Edward," the boy answered.

"Well, Mr. Edward, my name is Liddlelite and my friend, Taylite, was caught by a fisherman. He stuck Taylite in a glass jar so that his light would attract some of Shallowpond's biggest fish," continued the firefly. "But the fisherman left him floating in the jar out in the middle of the water, and I don't know how to rescue him. Taylite is the one who saw where the squishberries went," recalled Liddlelite sadly.

Edward and the frog looked up and saw that indeed, they were close to the edge of Shallowpond, one of Wordishure's favorite fishing spots. And sure enough, floating out in the pond was a glass jar with a glowing light coming from inside.

"He is way out there," observed the frog. "I'll swim out and bring your friend back in."

"Don't do that," warned Liddlelite. "Hookie LePike lives in these waters, and he loves frog legs!"

"Gulp," swallowed the frog nervously. "M..mm..maybe Edward can help!" The frog pointed toward Edward's pocket.

Edward checked in his pocket for his perfect skipping stone. He thanked God that he had another chance to use it, especially to help someone. Maybe the skipping stone was a blessing after all. Edward reached down into his pocket, found the stone, and held it up.

"That is a perfect skipping stone," remarked Liddlelite.

At that, Edward stepped ankle-deep into the water, bent his

arm back....and threw! "Tap, tap, tap," it skipped towards the glass jar, and then... "tap, tap, crash!" The stone had broken the jar and Taylite began to flitter back towards the shore.

"Thank you! Thank you, and God bless you," said Taylite to Edward and the frog. "I never thought I'd be glad to see a frog!"

"You're welcome, I think..." laughed the frog.

"Can you tell us where the basket of squishberries went?" asked Edward.

"Sure," replied Taylite, "they are hidden over there, behind the burping bush."

Just then a loud burp came from the bush that Taylite had pointed to. Edward, the frog, and the two fireflies hurried to the bush and slowly peered around its branches. Sitting behind it was a goose with a bloated tummy and squishberry juice all over his beak.

"Honx the Goose!" the frog exclaimed.

"Sam Phibian!" replied the goose.

At the sight of his friend, Honx, the frog's memory had been restored.

"You two know each other?" asked Edward excitedly.

"As a matter of fact, yes," declared Sam the frog. "I remember every bit now. You see, Honx and I were floating out in the middle of Lil' Valley Pond when he saw your basket of squishberries, which had been left alone. Honx loves squishberries..."

"I sure do," honked Honx.

"He swam over to get them, and when I cried out for him to stop, a stone hit me on top of my noggin' and I lost my memory," recalled Sam.

"Oops," added Edward. "Sorry again."

"I'm sorry too," Honx chimed in.

"Forgiveness can never truly happen without repentance, Honx," said Sam wisely.

"Oh, I know," revealed the goose. "That's why I picked more squishberries...look!"

Honx was right, the basket was overflowing now!

"I discovered that this bush was loaded with them," announced Honx joyfully. "After I loaded up the basket, I decided to snack on some of the leftovers!"

Honx waddled over with the basket and set it before Edward. It was four times fuller than before! Everyone let out a cheer, and they all thanked the Lord for their new friends. Edward even invited them all to Fellowship Church to hear singing, preaching, and to share Grandma's squishberry pancakes.

The Three Princesses of Wordishure

"Likewise, I say unto you, there is joy in the presence of the angels of God over one sinner that repenteth."
Luke 15:10

In the heart of Wordishure sat a beautiful castle. It was a beacon of hope for those who sought answers from the King. It was also the home of his Queen and three beautiful daughters. These princesses were well known and highly regarded for their tender hearts and charitable nature.

The eldest was Princess Irelynd. She loved to sing. Whenever she sang a song about Jesus, the animals would come from all around just to listen. The second oldest was Princess Tara, who God blessed with a wonderful imagination. She painted the most beautiful pictures in all of Wordishure. The third and youngest was Princess Ashtyn. She loved to plant flowers. Her favorite was the Hia Rose, which she planted all over the land.

One day, the three princesses were playing together when a servant came in and asked them to come meet a visitor in the royal courtyard. The were excited about having a visitor, so they brushed their hair and tidied up their things (whoever heard of a messy princess?).

Because it was the King's naptime, the three princesses had to tiptoe down long corridors passing large rooms, until they reached the courtyard. That's where they saw the visitor who was patiently waiting for them. When the boy saw the princesses' approach, he walked up to greet them. His light gray cloak swept the cobblestones of the courtyard as he stepped up to the princesses and bowed down before them.

"Hello Princesses," greeted the boy.

"I've seen you before," noted Princess Irelynd. "You're a new member at Fellowship Church."

"That's right," he affirmed. "My name is Philip. My sister Abby and I saw you sitting with the King and Queen during Sunday's service. My family just moved to Bigwater Falls," he explained.

"Welcome to Wordishure Castle. I'm Princess Irelynd, and these are my two sisters, Princess Tara and Princess Ashtyn."

"It's nice to meet you," said Princess Tara.

"Abby shared some of her candy with me at church, can you give her this for me?" asked Princess Ashtyn, holding out a bright red flower to Philip.

"Thank you," replied Philip, taking the flower.

"It's a Hia Rose, the most precious flower in all of the Kingdom," remarked Ashtyn.

"Does Abby have any more candy?" asked Princess Tara.

"Yes. But she is missing," said Philip sadly. "I have come to ask for your help in finding her."

All three princesses agreed to help their new friend.

"We'll ask our parent's if we can help. It's always good to ask permission first," insisted Princess Irelynd. "Do you have any thoughts on where she might be?"

Philip reached into his cloak and pulled out a map of Wordishure. He unrolled the map on the cobblestones and pointed to a drawing of a bridge.

"The last time I saw her, she was picking Sweet Lillies by Rickety Bridge," recalled Philip. "She wanted to wear a special flower in her new bonnet at church on Sunday. But she has not returned, and if we don't return home before sunset, our parents will be worried."

Rickety Bridge was the wobbliest bridge in Wordishure. It was an old cracked up wooden footbridge that was in need of repair. Before they left, the princesses found their mother, the Queen, and asked if it was okay if they helped their new friend.

"That is very sweet girls," the Queen said. "But make sure you return home for supper, I am making a big meal for the

King. He is always hungry when he wakes up from his nap."

The girls gathered their new friend and started on their journey. It was a long walk, but the princesses took Philip along the scenic route, showing him all of their favorite places. They jumped over Laughing Brook, found a path through Puzzlewood Maze, and twirled in circles through Whirly Bird Meadow (where they had to wait until they weren't dizzy anymore). Wherever they went, Princess Ashtyn made sure to plant fast-growing flower seeds, that way they would have a trail of flowers to follow on the way back home.

"There's some Sweet Lillies," said Princess Ashtyn, pointing to the flowers growing by Rickety Bridge.

"This is where I last saw Abby," recalled Philip as they approached the bridge.

"Halt!" came a stern voice from the bridge.

It was the Bridge Mizer, the keeper of Rickety Bridge. His long white beard grew over the front of his patched up uniform. Although Bridge Mizer was very old, he dutifully kept guard over his beloved bridge.

"Nobody comes through here without paying the

rickety toll!" he warned them, raising one his thick white eyebrows.

"But we didn't bring any money," worried Princess Irelynd.

The old man grinned and stood his ground, crossing his arms across his chest. "My bridge may be old and shaky, but it still serves a great purpose. How do I know you're worthy to cross, eh? The toll must be paid!"

"Maybe I can help," said Princess Tara as she took out her trusted paint kit.

The Bridge Mizer watched curiously as she unrolled a piece of canvas and some paints that she always kept with her. She dipped her brush into some of the paints and then nimbly dabbed, brushed, blotted, and dabbed a little more. When Princess Tara had finished her painting, the picture was so beautiful, it nearly leapt off the canvas!

"Here you are," she said, handing the painting to the Bridge Mizer.

She had painted a picture of Rickety Bridge, but it no longer had any sags, cracks, or broken boards. The Bridge Mizer was pleased and wiped a single, joyful tear from his eye.

"This is wonderful, it's how I see the bridge in my heart. You have proven yourself worthy and may now pass over the bridge. And have a safe journey...little Abby is closer than you think."

"Have you seen her?" asked Philip.

"Yes, I have," remembered the Bridge Mizer nervously. "She has been kidnapped by Brimnibble, the hat-eating dragon. The great big dragon swooped down, ate my rickety hat, and nabbed Abby."

The Bridge Mizer then pointed to his balding head, "It was her bonnet for sure. Brimnibble loves bonnets! She must have flown her off to her Nibble Nest, which rests on the highest branch of the tallest tree in Uppatree Forest."

Legends of Brimnibble were known throughout all the land of Wordishure. In Squintville, it is said that the people now wear hats of broccoli, because the great green dragon does not like broccoli.

With his cloak waving in the wind, and shield in hand, Philip bravely stood before the three princesses and declared, "I'm not afraid of the dragon...plus, some of that candy was mine!"

They waved goodbye to the Bridge Mizer and crossed Rickety Bridge, running as fast as they could until they

reached Uppatree Forest. As they approached, they stopped to catch their breath. "Look," said Princess Tara. "A hat crumb trail!"

Princess Tara was right. Bits and pieces of chewed up hats formed a trail that led to a large tree.

"I can see the Nibble Nest," said Princess Ashtyn pointing to the branch where the nest was perched. "And there's Abby!"

"Hello everybody," a voice called down from the nest. "Can somebody come rescue me? I need help getting my candy down."

As they looked up, they could see Abby sitting on the side of the nest, holding a piece of her bonnet and a bag of candy. As she waved to them, a few candy wrappers floated down and landed by the children's feet.

"Hurry, before Brimnibble comes back!" shouted Abby, before tooting on a sugary Fizz-Whistle. "Or before all this candy is gone!"

"I'll help you Abby!" hollered Philip as he started to climb the tree.

Although he had won many tree climbing competitions in Bigwater Falls, Philip had never climbed one this high before. As he went higher, he became a little scared.

"Don't be scared, Philip," said Abby trying to reassure her brother. "Jesus once climbed a tree to save all of mankind."

This eased Philip's heart. Abby always trusted in the Lord, which helped him in times of self-doubt.

"Don't forget the Gum Droops!" Princess Tara called up to

them.

Philip reached the top and helped Abby climb down. When they got to the ground, Philip gave Abby a big hug.

Just then, a large shadow passed over all the children. As the children looked up, they could see Brimnibble as she circled in the air just above them. The wind from her wings caused a candy wrapper whirlwind that flew around the children! The great, green dragon landed with a ground shaking thump in front of them.

She snorted, patted her large belly and exclaimed, "I'm starving for hats! Delicious hair holders! Caps and derbs, I'll expose those combovers!"

"I'm not afraid of you, Brimnibble, I left my helmet at home!" proclaimed Philip, pointing to his head. "I'm going to close the lid on your hat-eating ways!"

The young boy stepped in front of the girls and held up his shield, bravely protecting them.

"This I've got to see," chuckled Brimnibble as she slowly approached the children.

Before brave Philip could stop her, Princess Irelynd stepped forward and began to sing. It was a song about Jesus, and how He bravely went to the Cross when He could have called ten thousand angels, but instead sacrificed Himself for us. Her beautiful voice carried throughout the whole forest as she sang of repenting from your sin and learning how to behave. This special song softened Brimnibble's heart. Tears welled in her eyes and a new look came upon her face.

"I don't want to misbehave anymore," the dragon cried. "I

want to hear more songs about Jesus, that's what I crave now!"

The dragon sat next to Princess Irelynd licked her hand. It felt like a cats tongue! Then Brimnibble apologized to Abby for being bad.

"I'm sorry I nibbled on your bonnet, Abby. Can I please have some candy too?" asked the dragon.

Abby used what was left of her bonnet to wipe away the dragon's tears and handed her a marshmallow sombrero.

"Thank you," said Brimnibble licking her lips. "These are my favorite. How did you know?"

"It was an easy guess," laughed Abby while pinching her nose. "You sure have terrible hat breath."

This made Brimnibble laugh too!

"Let's all eat some candy," suggested Princess Tara rubbing her tummy.

That's when they realized that it was almost time for supper.

"Oh no!" exclaimed Princess Irelynd. "We'll never make it back on time!"

"I can help," claimed Brimnibble as she lowered herself so the children could climb on her back. "But you'll have to show me the quickest way to the castle."

"Just follow the trail of flowers," asserted Princess Ashtyn as Brimnibble flew into the air.

Princess Ashtyn was right. Leading them to the castle was a beautiful trail of flowers. The children all waved to the Bridge Mizer as they passed over Rickety Bridge.

"God bless!" he shouted up to them, while holding his new picture and waving back.

When Abby waved, she nearly dropped a box of the Gooey Gobpoppers she was starting to open.

"Don't ruin your supper, Abby," reminded Princess Irelynd.

When the dragon landed them back at the castle, they saw the King and Queen waiting for them in the courtyard. They held onto their crowns as they watched Brimnibble land.

"It's okay, Daddy, Brimnibble has a brand new heart," said Princess Tara. "She won't eat your crowns."

The King and Queen let out a big sigh of relief. "You're all invited to supper," announced the King to his new guests. "The Queen has prepared a sumptuous meal, one fit for me!"

Then the King walked over, picked the children up off the dragon and set them down on the ground, one by one.

"I hope you didn't spoil your supper by eating lots of candy," said the Queen.

"Uh oh," said Abby, with chocolate all over her face.

After a good meal and plenty of games, Philip and Abby thanked the three princesses and let Brimnibble fly them home. Later, the princesses said their prayers, thanking God not only for Abby's safe return, but for Brimnibble's change of heart...and for candy!

The Treasure Map
Of Wordishure

"For where your treasure is, there will your heart be also."
Matthew 6:21

From the shadows emerged the little explorer. His heart
rate quickening as he approached the chest in the middle of
the dimly lit room. With each step closer, swirls of dust
would kick up around his feet. The floorboards creaked with
each step. With a slight grin he knelt down and ran a finger
through the dust that had built up on the old chest.

"Ahhhchhooo!" he sneezed.

"Is that you playing up in the attic, Micah," asked his mother.

"Yes, mom," he replied, twitching his nose as he unhooked the latch to the chest.

"I'm glad you've found grandfather's old things, but make sure you don't get your new shoes all dusty. Those are for church," she reminded him.

Micah looked down at his new shoes. They were made of the soft brown leather and were shiny from a fresh polish. The laces were neatly tied into knots like his father had just taught him. He couldn't wait to show all the people at church his fancy new shoes. He wiggled his toes and hummed to himself, slowly lifting the lid on the dusty old chest.

Inside were all sorts of treasures and memories from his grandfather's past. Old drawings, funny clothes, big shoes, and even some raggedy socks grandfather had worn a hole in! Digging farther into the chest, he an old book! It was thick and well worn, yet somehow familiar. It was held together with a piece of twine so some of the pages wouldn't fall out.

Micah decided that this new find deserved his undivided attention. "I know," he thought, "there's a tree down by the river. I can read this book while I relax in the shade."

"Ahhhchooo!" he sneezed again.

"Are you getting a cold, dear?" his mother called up again.

"No, ma'am," he responded. "It's just a bit of dust."

Carrying the old book he found, Micah walked down the

stairs from the attic and into the kitchen. "Can I go out and play?" he asked while rubbing his nose.

"Maybe some fresh air will clear the dust out," his mother said smiling and lovingly tousling his light brown hair. "Remember, Micah, going out can be fun, but the journey home is where we find true happiness."

Micah smiled, hugged his mother, and ran outside, jumping over the two steps leading down from the porch. He hurried toward Oldwood Creek, which was only a short run from the house. Micah knew the way well, for he had spent his whole life exploring the area and making friends with other local children. It was a little hot today, so he expected to see a friend or two down by the creek, fishing or resting under the big shade tree. He had heard others at church talking about building tree forts, so he hoped to build one here as well.

Slowing down to catch his breath, Micah started walking through some pickaberry bushes. This was his secret shortcut to the creek. Pickaberries were delicious when they were in season, but that was not for a while. He called them puckerberries when he ate them too soon, because they did not get sweet until autumn harvest. Approaching the edge of the bushes, he could see the shade tree down by the creek. He also spotted his little brother, Jonah, standing under the tree, scratching his head and looking a bit confused.

"Hello Jonah," greeted Micah smiling and waving.

"Oh. Hello, big brother," replied Jonah cheerfully. "What are you doing here?"

"I was going to ask you the same thing," replied Micah.

"It was a little hot today, so I came to soak my feet in the river, and nap under the shade tree," stated Jonah.

"Are those your new church shoes," asked Jonah. "I wish I could find mine."

Micah looked down at Jonah's bare feet. "What happened to your shoes and socks?"

Jonah shrugged his shoulders and pointed up the creek. "I took them off earlier when I decided to soak my feet in the stream. Later, when I came back, they were gone! Now I'm standing here all barefoot and fragrant!"

"I can help you look for them," volunteered Micah. "I don't want to see mom upset with you over losing your shoes and socks."

Micah began to look around hoping to find his brothers lost belongings. He set the old book he was holding on the ground and debated on where to start looking. "Perhaps they are by the tree stump where the carpenter ants live..."

"What is that?" interrupted Jonah, walking over to look at the book.

"It's an old book that belonged to grandfather," replied Micah. "Be careful, it's very old and precious."

Jonah picked up the book and started to undo the twine. As he fumbled with the knot, a piece of paper fell out from between the pages. It floated lazily to the ground. The paper was tattered, browning, and torn along one side. "It's a treasure map!" exclaimed Jonah as he knelt down to retrieve it. Both of the boy's eyes enlarged with excitement as Jonah carefully held it up by one corner.

"See," Jonah pointed to a marking on the map. "There are some Xs on a hill!"

Jonah immediately stood up and started running towards the creek. "I'll bet this creek will lead us right to it!" he exclaimed.

Micah, used to his brothers impulsiveness, smiled and ran after. "Maybe we should think about this," he stated. "We've never been down the river that far..."

But Jonah kept running, following the flow of the creek. "Wait up!" Micah shouted.

When he caught up with Jonah, it was because his brother had found a hidden trail in some of the thick, tall bushes that grew along the creek. "What is it," Micah asked. "The treasure?"

"It's a hidden trail!" exclaimed Jonah. "It's not a hill, but maybe there's a clue in here..."

Curiosity overtook the boys so they started down the thickly overgrown trail. Micah noticed little multi-colored threads here and there along the way. "I wonder what these could be?" he wondered out loud.

It wasn't long before they came to an opening in the thicket. Their eyes widened as a giant pile of socks came into their view.

"Wow!" said Jonah, stepping forward slowly.

The colorful pile was made up of thousands of socks and towered above their heads. After a few more steps forward, Micah and Jonah looked at each other, pinched their noses, and exclaimed, "PU!"

"I think these socks are all used," declared Micah, poking the pile with a stick he had found.

"Hey, watch the stick!" came a voice from inside the mound, where Micah had poked.

Micah and Jonah stepped back as a white, furry creature climbed out of the sock tower. After a stretch and a big yawn, the creature walked up to them. It was long, slender, had big dark eyes. It also wore a clothespin on its nose!

"You're a sock weasel!" proclaimed Jonah.

"My name is Argyle," the weasel said in a nasally voice. "Can't anyone take a nap in an odorific pile of socks without being poked by a stick?"

"We're sorry," Micah replied. "But we're on a quest to find the greatest treasure in all of Wordishure!"

"Then you've found it!" declared Argyle triumphantly as he pulled out a sock and placed it on his head like a cap. "Welcome to Argyle's Sockpile Palace!"

"Eeeww," said Micah.

"Hey, that's my sock on your head!" observed Jonah.

"Does it have your name on it?" questioned Argyle with a smug look.

"As a matter of fact, it does..." replied Jonah pointing to the brim of the sock, which spelled out JONAH upside down. His mom had written his name on it to keep him from losing them.

Argyle tried to read the sock while it was still on his head and stumbled backwards. However, Micah ran up and caught him before he could trip.. "You have to take it off before reading it, silly."

"Oops," blushed the sock weasel. "I suppose you'll be wanting it back then," he replied a little sadly.

"I'd like them both back, please," said Jonah. "Before I get cold feet."

"I'll be right back," said Argyle after handing Jonah the sock off his head. "I was using the other one as part of a hammock!"

Argyle quickly dove back into the mound of socks, and then emerged with the matching one. "Thank you very much," said Jonah as he sat on the ground to put his socks back on. "Where did you get them?"

"I found them on the shore by the creek," answered Argyle. "They were left abandoned by an a tree stump."

"I knew I shouldn't have left for a pickaberry snack," Jonah sighed. "I lose more shoes and socks that way!"

"Tsk Tsk," buzzed a small voice from nearby.

"Did someone say missing shoes?" buzzed another small voice.

Micah, Jonah, and Argyle all looked at each other, and then walked over to a bush nearby. They saw two small insects sitting on a Pickaberry vine and sipping some tea.

"Those are Chatterbugs!" said Micah.

"I'll say," said Argyle. "They talk more then the Yakkity Yaks that graze over on Prattler's Field."

Chatterbugs lived throughout all of Wordishure. They resembled grasshoppers, but had large ears, slight overbites, and loved to drink tea. They were well known for their love of chit-chatting, chewing the fat, flapping their gums, and the pulling of ears. And these two were no exception!

"I say young lads, you're looking a bit lost. Is there something that we may help you with?" questioned one of the Chatterbugs.

"Oh, right-O," the other one chimed in.

"I've never talked to a Chatterbug before," said Micah as he knelt down to their level.

"Would you like some Pickaberry tea?" the first one asked politely.

"No thank you, sir." Micah said. "We're not thirsty."

"Tut Tut," said the second Chatterbug.

"Did I say something wrong," asked Micah, feeling a little perplexed.

"No, no, dear child. That is my name, Tut Tut. And this is my palley-o-chum-mate, Tsk Tsk."

"I'm Micah, and this is my brother, Jonah. We're looking for the greatest treasure in all of Wordishure!"

"And my shoes," added Jonah.

"Wonderful," shouted Tsk Tsk excitedly. "This will be the talk of the land!"

27

"A tale of Wordishure to be told repeatedly through all generations," added Tut Tut, tapping teacups with Tsk Tsk in a toast.

Micah and Jonah smiled at each other as the Chatterbugs continued to buzz about the grandness of their adventure. "It's hard to find treasure with no shoes on," interrupted Jonah.

Tut Tut then leaned forward and with a hushed tone, whispered, "It just so happens that Tsk Tsk has just heard something through the vine..."

All three of them turned to look at Tsk Tsk, who was listening to a cup-like device that was attached to the end of a Pickaberry vine.

"Hold it right there, Argyle!" said Tsk Tsk, dropping the cup and vine. He stood up and pointed at Argyle, who when nobody had noticed, started tiptoeing away.

"Who me?" asked Argyle, twitching his whiskers.

"It seems our cousin, Pip Pip, was buzzing around the creek today and saw Argyle joyfully waving around some new socks," revealed Tsk Tsk.

"That we know," replied Jonah, pointing to his sock-covered toes.

"Can I deduce there was also a pair of shoes?" asked Tut Tut smugly.

"Top-notch reasoning, Tut Tut. Brilliant work," said Tsk Tsk as they tapped teacups again.

When the two boys turned to look at Argyle, a deep booming voice spoke to them from a nearby tree, "Are these your shoes?"

Everyone looked up. Just over their heads, sitting on a large branch and kicking his shoe-covered feet, was a great big owl wearing horn-rimmed glasses. "I love shoes, but I can't figure out how to tie the laces," he said in a frustrated tone.

"Cahoots the owl!" Tut Tut said. "I should have known you and Argyle were together on this!"

Cahoots and Argyle had been friends a long-time. One liked shoes and the other liked socks, so they were the perfect pair. Cahoots flew down from the tree and landed on the ground by Micah. Cahoots was a giant owl, easily twice Micah's size. The bird looked silly trying to walk around with his claws barely fitting into Jonah's small-untied shoes.

"You have nice shoes," Cahoots said to Micah. "And they are tied so neatly. Can you teach me how to tie my shoes?"

"I'll teach you how to tie your shoes if you give Jonah his shoes back," Micah said.

"That would be wonderful," Cahoots replied. "But then I won't have shoes to tie...finder's keeper's ya' know."

It was at that moment Micah remembered finding his grandfather's old shoes that were still in his attic. He also remembered that where your treasure is, there will your heart be also. Micah liked the idea of helping Cahoots find a treasure of his own.

Micah told the owl about his grandfather's shoes and proposed a trade. Cahoots liked the idea and hooted with joy. Argyle, anxious to help, beckoned Micah, Jonah, and Cahoots over to a large basket of collected socks. "You could fly them

home," said Argyle, emptying most of the socks from the basket. "I'd be honored if you used my trusty sock basket!" After climbing in and putting clothespins on their noses, Micah and Jonah said goodbye to their new friends, Argyle and the Chatterbugs. The two boys agreed to come back and let them know when they found the treasure.

Cahoots grasped the basket handle with his claws and flew the boys high into the air. Micah and Jonah held onto the basket tightly as they rose high up into the sky above Oldwood Creek. They could see for miles in every direction! Micah even saw Wordishure Castle way off in the distance.

"There's our house," said Micah, pointing out the way. "There's our mom!"

Micah's mom was surprised to see them flying and waved to them from the front yard. Cahoots slowly glided down and set the basket next to her. Both boys climbed out and gave her a big hug. Jonah was just happy to be back on the ground, he liked being under the trees, not over them! It also gave him a chance to walk around in his old trusty shoes again.

Micah asked his mother if it was okay if they gave his grandfather's shoes to their new friend. His mother was pleased that Micah had listened so well in his Sunday School class. Micah ran up into the attic, and grabbed the shoes from the old chest. "Ahh choo!" he sneezed again, scattering more dust about. He even remembered the moldy socks to take to Argyle too! Soon, Cahoots was walking about happily with the shoes on his feet, all neatly tied as Micah had taught him.

Micah's mother smiled as she watched them all head down to the big shade tree by Oldwood Creek. Jonah thought that Cahoots could help them figure out the treasure map. After all, owls are well known for their wisdom. Jonah carefully held up the map by the corner showing Cahoots the Xs.

"Do you know what these Xs are?" asked Micah. "Flying above the land must give you a great bird's eye view of where to look."

Cahoots adjusted his horn-rimmed glasses and studied the map that Jonah was still holding up by its corner. "Hmmm..." said the owl. "Where exactly did you get this map?"

"It fell out of this book," Micah said, picking up the book from under the shade tree.

Cahoots smiled and sat down with the book. He tugged the twine free with his beak and opened it. Then Micah and Jonah could see what was in the book. It was God's Word!

Micah remembered his grandfather reading it to them at night. Jonah was just a baby, and Micah remembered the parables. He also loved the "thee's" and "thou's" of the old Biblical English.

"It's a Bible map," Cahoots explained.

Micah then realized what happened. "Jonah, you were holding the map sideways," he commented, jumping to his feet. "It's a map of Calvary!"

Cahoots turned the map so they were reading it correctly. The three Xs were really the three crosses on Calvary's hill. This reminded them of Jesus's sacrifice of love.

"Then it was a treasure map after all!" declared Jonah.

Micah, Jonah, and Cahoots took the book and sat down on the grass under the big shade tree, thankful for their discovery. They now held the treasured Bible in their hands and planned to share the riches with all their new friends.

Bigby The Giant of Wordishure

"I love them that love me; and those that seek me early shall find me."Proverbs 8:17

Deep in the heart of Meadowvalley Glenn lived a giant named Bigby. He was known throughout all of Wordishure, not only for his notable size, but also for his playful spirit. Bigby was as tall as a house and strong as an elephant! He once lifted a tree fort up into a tree with his friends still in it!

Bigby also loved to attend Fellowship Church, even though he barely fit inside. Bigby liked helping the Pastor. He even volunteered to play the lead role in the church's upcoming children's play, "Daniel in the Lions Den." Bigby couldn't wait to find out who else was going to be in the play, so he asked the Pastor.

"The church mice, Colby, Pepper, and Jack, are in it with you," answered the Pastor, looking up at him. "They're supposed to be rehearsing, but I can't seem to find them anywhere."

Bigby loved the idea of being on a mission, so he volunteered his services. "I'm having lunch with my friends Filmore and Turner," he stated. "I'll ask them to help me search for the mice."

After departing Fellowship Church Bigby met his friends Turner the chameleon and Filmore the cat. They decided to start their search on Walkdown Trail. There were lots of places to hide there, and Bigby knew the mice were apt to find a little place to sequester themselves and practice their lines.

Along the way the trio decided to play a game. Bigby loved games and couldn't resist playing at least one. "Let's play 'Seek the Lost'," said Turner, as he ran down the trail in front of his two friends.

Turner was Bigby's smallest friend. The chameleon never learned to control his color changes and had taken to wearing camouflage. "It's my favorite game!" Turner continued.

"Okay," answered Bigby. "but we must be quick if we want to help the pastor."

"And get some lunch!" exclaimed Filmore the cat.

"It will be real quick, I promise." Turner answered while making a cross over his heart.

"Seek the Lost" was Bigby's favorite game. First, you covered your eyes. Then, as you counted to ten, your friends would find a place to hide. After you finished counting, you had to seek them out and call them home.

"We always play that, Turner," said Filmore who had stopped to rest on a fallen tree. "I'm much easier to find than you are."

Filmore was right. It was easier to spot a plump black and white furred cat in the woods than a small lizard dressed up in camouflage.

Turner, who was now too excited to listen, scuttled farther away down Walkdown Trail. "I just thought of the best hiding place," he said to the cat before disappearing off into some colorful brush.

"All right, let's play," sighed Filmore as he stood up, "but give me a generous head start, Bigby."

Bigby smiled and crouched down by a nearby Oakypine tree. Covering his eyes, he could hear Filmore crunching through the leaves looking for a place to hide.

"One....two...three..." Bigby counted. Bigby loved numbers. He hoped to learn more as he got older, so he'd always know his proper age.

"Four....Five...Six..." he continued.

"Seven....Eight..." He couldn't hear anything now; only the soft breeze as it blew through the small leaves of the

Oakypine trees.

"Nine and ten!" Bigby finished counting and stood up.

"Ouch!" he exclaimed as he bumped his head on a branch.

"I once was blind, but now I see," Bigby traditionally called out as he began to "Seek the Lost." Usually the giant boy was quick at finding Filmore. If his bulbous shape and white fur did not give him away, then it was the sound of the cats purring or rumbling tummy.

Bigby searched high in the trees and under a few giant boulders. Sometimes Turner would squeeze underneath them. Bigby used his big lungs to blow away piles of leaves that his friends may have hidden under. As the leaves descended down through the air, Bigby heard giggling. Turner always giggled whenever anyone came close enough to find him.

"I've found you, Turner!" exclaimed Bigby, while looking inside a gathering of Cactickles. Cactickles were a common plant that grew in Wordishure. Instead of being thorny, they grew small feathers that tickled whoever touched them.

"I knew I should have tried someplace else," Turner giggled while scratching his feet where the feathers had tickled him. "But I never thought you'd look in here."

"Seek the lost wherever you can find them," Bigby said wisely while doing a slight bow, "those are the rules."

"I hope Filmore does better with his hiding place," chuckled Turner as the giant lifted him up onto his shoulder.

"Help! Help!" came the sound of Filmore's voice from off

in the woods.

"Uh oh," Turner said. "I think Filmore may have bitten off more than he can chew. I hope he isn't stuck between two trees again."

Bigby started into the woods towards the direction of Filmore's voice. "Help! Bigby! Turner!" he cried out again. Bigby ran through the trees making big booms with each thunderous footstep. Leaves fell, birds flew from branches , and stones were shook loose. By the time the young giant came to a halt at the bottom of a large, clover-covered hill, the woods looked quite a mess.

Now, this wasn't just any hill; it was Ontoppa Hill, the highest point in all of Wordishure. Bigby hoped Filmore had not climbed up, but he heard Filmore cry out again "Up here, Bigby!"

Bigby carried Turner up the hill as fast as he could. When he reached the top he saw Filmore dancing around waving his paws into the air. "Big bee, big bee!" he warned as his friends approached.

Filmore was right. The cat was surrounded by a swarm of really big bees! "His paws are covered with honey!" Turner noticed, quickly approaching their friend. When the bees saw the giant approach they stopped swarming around Filmore, who, in turn, ran to hide behind Bigby. "You could at least stop eating the honey while you're trying to run" commented Turner as Filmore peeked out from around his large friend.

"But it's so delicious," panted Filmore, and then shrugged his shoulders. "I thought the hive was abandoned."

"You shouldn't bee a finders keeper," joked Bigby.

The giant turned to the large bee flying in front of him and apologized, "We're sorry. Our friend didn't know anybody lived in the hive."

"Thank you Mr. Giant," nervously stated the bee after sizing up the large boy. "My name is Bix, I'm a Humblebee."

"We try to make the sweetest honey in all of Wordishure," the bee continued. "Our hive wasn't abandoned, we were down the hill collecting nectar. Every day we humbly go collecting it from four-leaf clovers, so our honey is extra sweet. We're always willing to share, but your friend almost ate it all!"

"I'm sorry, I've got plenty of honey in some jars at home. I should have been more thoughtful," interjected Filmore with a heartfelt apology. All of a sudden his ears perked up and he grinned, "I know! I'll go home to grab the honey and help you refill your nest!"

"That'll get my hive buzzing again!" Bix grinned.

"Where is your hive?" Turner asked, looking around.

The Humblebees let out a collective gasp before flying over to where the hive used to rest in the tree. "Oh no!" Bix exclaimed. "Our hive is missing!"

They frantically looked around until Bigby noticed a trail

of honey running along the ground that led down to the bottom of the hill. "My giant footsteps must have shaken the hive loose from the branch. It must have rolled down the hill!"

"Now we don't have a home," declared Bix sadly to the Humblebees.

"Lord willing, we'll seek your lost home," Bigby told the large bee. "And then we'll refill it to overflowing!"

"You must be a big bee at heart," said Bix to the giant, feeling a little better.

"This should be fun!" said Turner, climbing down from Bigby's shoulder onto the ground. The little chameleon straightened out his shirt, tightened his belt and said, "First the church mice, and now the hive. We really are seeking the lost!"

The three friends reassured the Humblebees and started down the hill in their quest for the bees' hive. Filmore felt guilty about what he had done and couldn't wait to make things right again. They followed the honey trail downward through a small grove of Oakypine trees. "Look," Turner said, pointing to a cave at the bottom of the hill. "The trail of honey goes right into that cave!"

Filmore, who is scared of the dark, nervously stated. "A cave? B..b..but it's so dark in caves...".

"Don't be a scaredy cat," said Turner sternly. "Look, it's just a little dark — there's probably nothing in there."

As they approached, they could see that the cave entrance was blocked. "The trail of honey leads right under this rock.

Now what do we do?" asked Filmore as he sat himself on old log that was next to the opening. "All hope is lost, it's been covered by a giant stone!"

"I can move it," said Turner flexing his tiny green arm into a muscle.

"Whatever thou doest, do it quickly," Filmore joked while patting his belly. "We still need to find lunch."

Bigby walked along the front of the cave moving his hands all along the rocky surface. "I think I may be able to move this," he stated while tapping his finger on his chin.

"It must have fallen down when you shook the ground trying to rescue me," said Filmore.

Bigby nodded in agreement. "Stand aside guys, I'm going in," Turner stated impatiently before placing his hands on the big stone.

That's when a loud roar came from behind the large stone. "Or maybe not!" he yelped, turning a bright shade of yellow. Turner whirled around and leapt into Filmore's lap, knocking him backwards off the log.

"What was that!" they exclaimed nervously, peeking out from behind the log.

"I don't know," said Bigby, as he placed his ear to the giant stone. "But it's definitely coming from inside this cave!"

"M...M...Maybe we can find an abandoned hive somewhere else..." stuttered Filmore. "Then we can leave this place be."

"Helping yourself to something that doesn't belong to you is how we got into this mess," Bigby replied

Filmore's heart sank. He knew Bigby was right, and that others were counting on him to make up for what he did. "Sometimes doing the right thing isn't easy," sighed Filmore, walking up to Bigby.

"Amen to that," Turner sighed while slowly changing back

41

into green.

"The solution to our problem is to roll away the big stone," explained Bigby as he knelt on the ground. "Then we'll find what we've been looking for."

All three friends took a minute to sit down together and pray. They asked God to give them the strength to move the stone, rescue the Humblebee's home, and find the missing church mice. After making their request, the young giant stood up and walked to the cave entrance. He placed one hand on each side of the stone. Filmore and Turner stood back and watched their mighty friend as he tried to roll the stone away from the entrance.

Bigby pulled at the stone with all his might, hoping to shift its position. Then, as he looked down, he could see that Filmore and Turner had joined him in trying to dislodge it. Filmore's fur stood on end and Turners color changed to a deep shade of red as the stone finally gave way under the strength of all three friends.

Exhausted, they collapsed in front of the large cave entrance and waited to catch their breaths. "Phew," Filmore said, laying on his back and looking up to the sky. "I guess we truly can bear one another's burdens," he stated, struggling to get back up.

After catching his breath, Bigby helped Filmore back on his feet. They moved to the front of the cave entrance and peered in. The walls of the cave were covered with drawings. They also saw a large tunnel that led further down into the cave.

"What are these drawings of?" asked Turner, pointing at the walls.

"They look familiar," said Bigby as he crouched to enter the cave.

"They are pictures of you Filmore," Turner exclaimed. "Really big cats!"

"No, silly. These are drawings of lions," observed Filmore.

All three friends looked at each other at the same time and gasped, "Lions!"

Bigby stepped in front of Filmore and Turner just as they were about to run out into the woods. "Hold on you two," Bigby said calmly, "Do you remember in the Bible how Daniel trusted in God to keep the lion's mouths shut? We should trust the Lord, He'll be our strength."

As the giant finished more loud roars came from the tunnel. "Alright, Bigby," Turner said, looking around nervously. "I guess this is our opportunity to seek and trust Him."

Bigby smiled, ducked his head down, and led both his shaky but newly determined friends into the cave tunnel. All three crept quietly and cautiously, hoping not to disturb any ferocious lions.

The roars got louder and louder, but their faith in God held strong. Bigby suddenly came to a stop, then pointed to a light coming from an opening up ahead. They slowly approached the opening and one by one they peeked their heads around the corner. The roaring abruptly stopped.

"Hello, Bigby," spoke a familiar voice.

"Hello," said Bigby, letting out a huge sigh of relief. Standing in front of him were the three small mice that lived onboard Fellowship Church. They were dressed in the tiniest lions costumes Bigby had ever seen.

Filmore and Turner sighed with relief as well and approached the church mice. Their names were Colby, Pepper, and Jack. Filmore always enjoyed listening to them whenever they sang a special song during church service. Their high voices were fun and melodious.

"We've been looking all over for you! You three look ferocious in those costumes," laughed Turner as they met with them.

"We're playing the parts of the lions in the church play" said Colby leaping around like a lion in his costume.

"I know," said Bigby. "I'm in it too. The pastor was hoping I'd find you, that way we could rehearse."

"That sounds wonderful," Jack replied. "This cave has been a great to practice our roars in!"

Jack let out a roar and it picked up volume from the cave's echo, amplifying it, making him sound like a mighty lion.

"Were we convincing?" asked Pepper as she sat on a nearby rock, pretending to clean her paw.

"Oh, I wasn't too scared" Filmore said, blushing.

"I was," admitted Turner. "You guys are good!"

"Did you see the cool drawings we made on the cave walls? Don't they look real?" asked Colby.

"They look hundreds of years old," winked Bigby. "When pastor asked me to play Daniel, I didn't realize I really would end up in the lions den!"

"Be careful, Bigby. Remember, we're the hungriest lions in all of Wordishure!" said Pepper playfully while rubbing her belly.

At that moment, Filmore's stomach rumbled loudly. "Now that's a real lion's roar!" laughed Jack as Colby dove behind him.

Everyone laughed and started practicing making some roaring noises themselves. That's when Bigby spotted the beehive lying in the corner. "It's the Humblebees home!" Bigby exclaimed, picking up the hive. "We should return it to them before they get too worried."

After saying goodbye to the church mice, they left the cave and started walking back up Ontoppa Hill. Filmore felt exhausted. "I sure could use some honey," he purred, giving Bigby his best sad eyes.

Bigby shook his head and smiled, "Oh Filmore, what am I to do with thee?"

They were still giggling about this when they approached the Humblebees who were waiting at the top of the hill. The happy bees buzzed around joyfully. They even let out three cheers when Bigby placed their home back into the tree where it belonged.

"Thank you," Bix exclaimed. "You're welcome to Ontoppa Hill whenever you like," said Bix.

"Now we can go back to my house for the honey I promised," said Filmore to the bees.

The Humblebees, being humble, graciously accepted

Filmore's offer. They even agreed to come to church and to watch the play. "We've never been to church before," Bix said as he flew around Bigby's head. "Are you sure that will be okay?" asked Bix.

"Your presence will be sweeter than honey," joked Bigby as he started to walk down the hill. "But please, Bix, watch where you sit."

The bee laughed and wiggled his stinger.

"How will I know when to be there?" asked Bix.

"Just listen for the church bell. I ring it loudly every Sunday morning," Bigby answered.

Turner climbed down off Bigby's shoulder and ran ahead of them on the trail. "Before we get to Filmore's, does everyone want to play a game?" he asked.

Filmore, knowing what the answer would be, replied, "Seek the Lost?"

Bigby smiled at all his friends and said, "We sure have, Filmore, we sure have."

The giant had now come to the realization that this adventure was not about finding the church mice or even the bee's home. If was about finding lost souls and inviting them to hear more about Jesus Christ

The Tree Fort
of Wordishure

*"Every good gift and every perfect gift is from above,
and cometh down from the Father of lights,
with whom is no variableness, neither shadow of turning."*
James 1:17

Sitting high up in his tree fort that overlooked Springwater Lake, Gideon watched the sun slowly rising over Wordishure. He appreciated the way the light made everything come to life.

As Gideon sat on the edge of the doorway, he looked

down at his bare feet and wiggled his toes. Gideon loved to walk barefoot through the grass because it was cool and soft.

"Good morning, Gideon," came a deep but slow voice from right under him.

Gideon climbed halfway down the ladder, and facing the tree, replied "Good morning Fordywinx."

The tree smiled and yawned while stretching out some branches. Gideon remembered the day he met Fordywinx, the Sleeping Willow tree. It was on a day that he was using his naptime invention that he called Slumbershades. They were a pair of glasses with the lenses painted black so the light wouldn't get into his eyes. This helped him nap better on sunny afternoons. Gideon was at the lake collecting bubbles for his next invention when he decided to take a nap under the shadiest tree possible. That's when the Sleeping Willow noticed his Slumbershades and remarked that he wanted a pair.

The old tree and the little boy became fast friends. Fordywinx even agreed to let Gideon build a tree fort in his upper branches, so he could work on more inventions. Word of the upcoming tree fort spread throughout all the land of Wordishure. Children from far and wide came to help build it. They had so much fun they decided to join up with Gideon and form a brave band of Tree Scouts. Their largest member, Bigby the Giant, helped the club by placing the fort into the tree.

Gideon and the Tree Scouts spent many hours in the fort playing games and telling stories. Gideon loved being a Tree

Scout. Besides meeting all sorts of new friends, it taught him to be good a steward of all God's Creation. Being a Tree Scout meant spending time learning knot tying, tree climbing, and map reading. But for Gideon, it meant watching the sunrise before starting work on his inventions.

As Gideon talked to Fordywinx, he pointed at his feet and said, "I'm working on an alarm system for my shoes."

He reached down into the pouch that he wore attached to his belt and pulled out a piece of string with some bells tied to it. "I just tie them on the laces. The chimes will let everyone know where I am," he said, rattling the bells in front of the sleepy-eyed willow tree.

"Try not wear to them at nap time," yawned Fordywinx. "Or I'll never get any rest!"

"That will be my next invention," declared Gideon as he pulled out a notepad and scribbled his new idea. "I'll make earplugs for trees!"

"I'll stick to counting sheep, thank you," said the tree, pointing a branch towards the sheep that were grazing in a field a short distance away. "Counting my wooly friends in Shepard's Field always gets me sleepy."

"You can count on me!" the little boy replied as he stood straight up on the ladder and saluted. "A Tree Scout's oath is His Word!"

"Toot!" came a loud noise from behind Gideon. "Toot! Toot! Toot!" It startled him so much that he nearly fell off the ladder! Fordywinx, steadied Gideon with one of his branches, so the boy wouldn't fall.

"Did I startle you?" came a familiar voice from the ground below. Gideon turned to look. Standing with a bugle in one hand was another Tree Scout, a young squirrel named Revelly. Gideon nicknamed him that because Revelly marched around with a bugle making all sorts of noise. Revelly the squirrel lived in the Clankabang tree just over Shepard's Field. Revelly wore his Tree Scout uniform all prim and proper. He was very good at tree climbing, and that's how he achieved his first Tree Scout merit pin. Revelly was reddish-brown, with a big fluffy tail that straightened out whenever he would trump on his horn.

Standing next to Revelly was his little sister Jubilee, who also was a Tree Scout. Jubilee, or Jubah, as Gideon called her, had decorated her uniform with lots of pretty ribbons. She also wore one small, red Hia Rose in the small brown tuft of fur on her head. Jubilee loved to celebrate over the smallest occasion, and was really good at remembering all the special days in Wordishure. She also carried a blanket around with her because Revelly kept her up a lot with his bugling. She was always ready to catch a quick nap.

"Are we there yet?" asked Jubilee, while rubbing her eyes

and yawning.

"Shhh..." motioned Gideon, holding his finger to his lips. "It's still early and Fordywinx is trying to get a bit of shut-eye. You know the older ones need lots of rest, Revelly."

"Thank you," said the tree dozily, "Maybe that earplug invention isn't such a bad idea after all!"

"Sorry," whispered Revelly as he tiptoed up the ladder of the tree fort.

"Me too," added Jubilee as she ran to the tree and hugged him.

Soon they were all up in the tree fort sitting around a crate that they used for a table. In the middle of their makeshift table sat the Jingle Jar. They called it the Jingle Jar because it was large, glass, and jingled whenever someone pulled out a shiny merit pin. A Tree Scout earned a merit pin by doing helpful tasks or learning a skill.

"What's with the Jingle Jar, Jubah?" Revelly asked his sister as he tapped at its lid, making a tinny bang noise with each tap. "Did I earn a new pin?"

"Shh..." she hushed. "It's Fordywinx' birthday. I want to give him a Friendship merit pin."

"Fordywinx's birthday!" shouted Revelly, raising the bugle to his lips, "it's time to celebrate!"

Both Gideon and Jubilee leapt up and covered Revelly's mouth before he could blow into the bugle. "Shhh," Gideon shushed. "We have another surprise."

Revelly scrambled over to Gideon's invention table, and started picking up some of his contraptions, "Are you inventing something! C'mon, I can keep a secret!"

"Not this time," replied Gideon, walking over to the map of Wordishure hanging on the wall.

"Jubah has a great gift idea, but we have to go here to get it," noted Gideon as he pointed to the map. Revelly knew just where he was pointing.

"That's Bearfruit Island!" Revelly nervously remarked. "We shouldn't go there!"

"Why not?" wondered Jubilee.

"There's a monster on that island named Hubbub," claimed Revelly, making his paws into antler shapes on top of his head. As Revelly talked he took slow steps towards Gideon and Jubilee. "Hubbub has big antlers, and prowls around at night making all sorts of strange sounds!"

"Awwoooo!!" Revelly howled menacingly.

Jubilee quickly pulled her blanket over her head, then peeked her eyes out to look at Gideon. "Is this true?" she asked.

"Oh, I've heard the stories, but a Tree Scout never listens to gossip. Besides that, I'm more afraid of Revelly's bugle," chuckled Gideon. "We have to go to the island for the present, it is Fordywinx's birthday after all."

They all gathered around in a circle and asked God to bless them on their journey and thanked Him for their good friend Fordywinx. Gideon put some of his inventions into a backpack before quietly climbing down the ladder. They were careful not to wake the Sleeping Willow, who had dozed into a mild slumber.

Revelly wanted to bring the Jingle Jar, but Jubilee thought that would be too strong of a temptation for Revelly to make it jingle. After all, it's better to avoid temptation than face it. They tiptoed down to the edge of Springwater Lake and decided to follow the water's edge south until they arrived where they would be closest to the island. After traveling a while Gideon stopped to check the map of Wordishure.

Revelly, munching on an acorn, looked over the map with Gideon. "These are the tastiest acorns ever," he declared with full cheeks.

"Do you want one?" he asked while holding out an acorn for Gideon.

"No thanks, Revelly," answered Gideon. "I'll leave the acorns for you and Jubah."

As Gideon looked at the map, his tummy rumbled. He realized that he should find something to eat as well. On the map it showed that they were very close to a large grove of Grabapple trees, which grew in this area of Wordishure. Gideon loved Grabapples. They were bright blue, very sweet and extra juicy. They usually grew in the higher branches of the trees, so they were difficult to reach.

"Toot!" came a blast from Revelly's bugle. "Toot!" came the blast again. "Hey, Jubah, I've found more acorns!" exclaimed Revelly, as he hung upside down from a nearby tree branch.

Jubilee tied her blanket around her neck like a cape and climbed into the tree with her brother to pick some acorns. "Toot!" Revelly trumped again.

Just as soon as Revelly finished his bugling, two creatures emerged from the tall bushes that grew on either side of the tree. "What's all this racket about?" complained one as it rubbed its eyes. "Can't anybody get a nap around here?"

"I was dreaming of Grabapples," groaned the other as it let out a big yawn.

It was two Woodashoodas, small furry creatures not much bigger than Revelly or Jubilee. They were light brown with long arms, bright eyes, and bushy tails. Woodashoodas loved Grabapples, so Gideon knew that they must be close to where he could get lunch.

"Sorry to disturb your nap," said Gideon. "We didn't even know you were there."

"That's okay," replied the first one as he scratched behind his ear. "That bugle startled us and we nearly fell out of the hammocks in our Grabapple tree."

The two squirrels scrambled down the tree to introduce themselves to the Woodashoodas. "I'm Revelly, and this is Jubah, my sister. We're Tree Scouts. And we're on a quest with our friend Gideon!"

Revelly raised the bugle to his lips and was about to let out a trump when Jubilee stuffed an acorn into the end of the bugle. When Revelly tried to blow into it, his cheeks expanded real big and turned a bright red. "It's blocked! " he remarked.

"Thank you, Jubah. That would have been a loud one!" said the first Woodashooda. He pointed his thumb to his chest and stated, "I'm Dilly."

"And I'm Dally," said the second Woodashooda, as he adjusted the sleeping cap he was wearing. "What are you Tree Scouts doing so far away from your tree fort?"

"We're on a quest to get a birthday present for our friend Fordywinx, the Sleeping Willow tree," answered Jubilee.

"We're looking for Lullabirds, which are rare in Wordishure," Jubilee continued. "They sit perched in the trees singing praises to God and bringing rest to the weary. We hear there are some of these birds living on Bearfruit Island."

"Bearfruit Island?!" exclaimed Dilly as he nervously looked around in every direction. "That's where Hubbub lives!"

"You don't want to go there, no sir," Dally added. "Many strange sounds come from that place. Scary sounds!"

Suddenly, Gideon's stomach let out a loud grumble.

"It's him!" Dilly yelped, leaping up into Dally's arms, "It's Hubbub!"

"No, silly," Gideon laughed. "That was my tummy, I'm really hungry."

"I knew that," said Dilly as Dally set him down. "I wasn't scared..." he assured them while nibbling at his nails.

"We have some Grabapple's in our tree if you want some," Dally told Gideon. "But they are high up in the branches. Dilly and I ate all the ones we could reach."

"I can get some down for you," claimed Revelly as he tried to shake the acorn from his bugle. "I got a merit pin in tree climbing!"

"It's not that easy," explained Dilly. "Grabapple trees have smooth bark so they are hard to climb!"

"I have an idea," suggested Gideon. "Show us to the tree."

Gideon and his friends followed the Woodashoodas through the thick brush until they came to a large Grabapple tree. Gideon stared up in amazement at the sight of all the delicious and perfectly ripe Grabapples. He took off his backpack and set it in front of him. He dug through all sorts of strange looking items until he found the device that he was looking for. It was a set of bedsprings hooked onto a pair of old sandals.

The Woodashoodas watched with delight as Gideon slipped them onto his feet, and used them to bounce up into the tree. He picked armful after armful of tasty Grabapples.

"Let's celebrate!" cheered Jubilee, waving a twig baton as she led a small parade around the tree. Revelly marched behind her clacking two acorns together with each step.

"If we march around it seven times, maybe the rest of the Grabapples will fall!" proclaimed Revelly. "Just like Jericho!"

After the parade they sat down, gave thanks, and ate Grabapples for lunch. The Woodashoodas were pleased that Gideon enjoyed helping others. "Our long arms can only reach so far," said Dilly while lifting his arms in the air.

Gideon removed the springs from his feet and handed them to Dally. "Here you go, these are a gift."

"Thank you," replied Dally. "We love getting gifts."

"Jesus gave us the best gift of all," mentioned Jubilee as she chewed her Grabapple.

"We'd like His gift," said Dally. "If you teach us about it, we'll show you the quick way to Bearfruit Island."

"We sure can!" promised Revelly.

"If that's what you want, we sure will," Dilly said.

"Can it wait until tomorrow?" responded Dally, who enjoyed putting things off.

"Today is the day," explained Gideon. "The Lord must have brought us together, so we could help each other find our way."

The Woodashoodas learned about Jesus's gift of salvation, and turned their hearts over to Christ. They now had joyful spirits knowing that God had a special plan for them. After lunch they led the Tree Scouts down a trail that led them to the shore of Springwater Lake. From this point they could see the tiny island. It was quite beautiful, and not far away.

"Try not to wake Hubbub," warned Dilly. "He naps during the day, and goes out mostly before nightfall."

"There's no boat, Gideon," observed Jubilee. "Just this pile of broken sticks floating in the water."

"That's our raft!" Dilly stated proudly. "It was made of the finest dripsticks this side of Springwater Lake."

Dally nodded in agreement. "It's all yours. And don't worry about taking it, it only took us a minute to build this one!"

Gideon agreed. Not much planning went into this, but he was thankful for the raft, at least until they were halfway to the island and knee deep in water.

The three travelers waved to the Woodshooda's as soon as they reached the island. Gideon took a moment to remove his shoes and squeeze the water from his socks. "I was hoping none of us would get cold feet!" he chuckled.

Suddenly the wind picked up and a low howling came from inside the grove of Bearfruit Trees.

"Wuh..whu..what was that?" stuttered Revelly as his eyes widened. "It's the monster!"

"Be brave, Revelly," encouraged Gideon. "We've got to find the Lullabirds."

Gideon put his finger to his lips and motioned for the others to follow. He was scared too, but Tree Scouts are brave, he reminded himself. They entered the trail and crept softly forward. If it were not for the monster, this would be a fun place to play, Gideon thought.

58

Walking farther down the trail they came upon a small clearing in the trees. They crouched down, joined hands, and slowly crept toward the noises. Appearing just a few paces ahead of them was the biggest Bearfruit tree on the whole island. "Wow," marveled Gideon as he looked up. In the tree's branches was a fort just like theirs! He also noticed a shadowy figure standing in the entrance. The monster was difficult to see, but it appeared to be covered in strange shapes. And it seemed to have antlers growing from its head.

"It's Hubbub!" exclaimed Revelly as he bravely stepped in front of his sister, protecting her.

At that moment, a gust of wind blew strongly and the figure started to make noise like an out of tune instrument. The figure then started to fidget with something on its shadowy shape. The noise changed into musical notes! And as the wind picked up even more, the monster played a beautiful melody.

Being curious, Gideon stepped forward to get a better look. As the sun broke through the trees, it revealed Hubbub for what he really was, a little boy. The boy wore a strange coat with musical instruments sewn into it!

"Do you like my coat? It's one of my favorite inventions," said the boy as he walked down the wooden step from the tree fort.

Gideon noticed Hubbub's coat had a collection toot floots, ringalings, and even a stickwhistle!

"It's my 'Coat of Many Noises'," smiled Hubbub as he reached out to shake Gideon's hand.

59

"It sure is," Revelly sighed with relief, "we thought you were the monster everyone calls Hubbub!"

"I'm not a monster," replied Hubbub. "My name is James, and I'm an inventor!"

"Me too!" exclaimed Gideon.

After introducing themselves, Jubilee asked, "Is that one of your inventions on your head?"

"Yes, ma'am." admitted Hubbub. "I put a weather vane on my hat to show me which direction I'm headed. Now I know where I'm going, and thanks to my musical coat, everyone else does too!"

"What are you doing on this island," asked Gideon.

"I was born here," answered Hubbub. "My parents house isn't far. It was built upon the large rock that overlooks the lake. A long time ago I started working on my noisy inventions so my dad helped me build this tree fort. Now I can invent without disturbing my baby brother's naptime. He makes lots of noise too if you wake him up!"

"I hear that!" exclaimed Revelly, pulling out his bugle with the acorn still stuck in the hole.

Hubbub laughed. "I've got something for that."

He took out a shoehorn and plucked the acorn from the bugle. "There you go, Revelly, its good as new!"

"Thanks!" cheered Revelly before giving the horn a mighty "Toot!"

"We should call you Hubbub, Revelly!" winced Gideon while holding his fingers in his ears.

Hubbub laughed and said, "I love to celebrate every day

that God has made, that's why I made this coat. What are you three doing on this island?"

"We're going to celebrate our friend's birthday!" chimed Jubilee. "And we came here looking for the perfect gift."

"I've got lots of neat stuff in my tree fort. Maybe I can help," said Hubbub.

The children climbed the angled wooden steps up to the tree fort. Inside were many of the inventions that Hubbub was working on. There was also a map of Wordishure, an empty jar, and a cage that held the prettiest birds they had ever seen. The birds were white as snow with pink and blue feathers on each of their wings.

"Those are Lullabirds!" exclaimed Jubilee. "They're what we've been looking for!"

"I found them outside a little while ago," explained Hubbub. "They weren't feeling well, so I've nursed them back to health. I have trouble falling asleep at naptime, so I thought they might sing me to sleep. But they haven't made a peep since I brought them here."

Gideon walked over to the cage and petted one of the birds, which sweetly cooed as he touched its soft feathers.

"A caged bird never truly sings," Gideon informed Hubbub. "Freedom brings a merry heart, and a merry heart can't help but sing praises!"

"Let's set them free!" declared Hubbub.

"And I know just the place to do it," said Gideon as he picked up the cage.

"It will be Fordywinx's noon nap soon," said Jubilee,

gazing out the window. "We'll never get the Lullabirds there on time. And it's way too far to walk before sunset."

"Follow me," insisted Hubbub. "I've got an invention I'd like to try."

He quickly walked down the steps and waited for the others to follow. Gideon and Revelly each held one side of the Lullabird cage carrying it down the steps. Jubilee followed after them, putting her blanket over the cage so the birds would be calm on their trip. Hubbub led them through a hidden trail that led down to the opposite side of the small island. There they could see Hubbub's house. His mother waved to him from the window.

"Be home before supper, James." she said.

"Yes, ma'am," replied Hubbub, waving back.

He led them down the beach to a short dock. Sitting on the end of the dock was a small boat.

"Is it made from Dripsticks?" asked Revelly, testing it's buoyancy with his big toe.

"No, no, no," laughed Hubbub, "this was my dad's old fishing boat. He made it with Shurewood."

"The sail fell apart so I added a propeller and some peddles," he continued. "It's a good invention, but I'm afraid it may not be fast enough."

Suddenly, Gideon had an idea. He set down his backpack and reached in. He grabbed the jar of bubbles that he collected. Pulling the jar out he held it up for the others to see. They were amazed at the number of bubbles that Gideon had collected.

"Those are perfect!" Hubbub said as Gideon handed him the jar of bubbles. Everyone climbed aboard as Hubbub opened the hatch door on the back. He then poured some bubbles onto the propeller, which immediately started to spin because of the popping. The boat sprang forward as the four children held on for the ride.

"It's a Bubblecraft!" shouted Revelly as they raced over the water towards the tree fort and Fordywinx.

"This is the best invention ever," Gideon told Hubbub. "We all make a great team!"

Hubbub's coat was making lots of noise as the Bubblecraft sailed along Springwater Lake. As the small boat glided smoothly across the water, it created large bubbles that Revelly tried to pop. Hubbub, remembering to look upward for guidance, checked his weathervane hat to make sure they were headed in the right direction. Reaching the shore by Fordywinx, they could see the Sleeping Willow was wide-awake and waving to them.

"What was that beautiful music?" asked Fordywinx.

"It's our new friends coat," answered Gideon as he walked up to the old tree. "His name is James, but we call him Hubbub. He's an inventor too!"

"God has certainly given him a gift," grinned the old tree.

"Speaking of gifts, we brought some for you!" remembered Gideon as he and Revelly set the blanket-covered cage in front of Fordywinx.

As Revelly pulled the blanket off the cage, the children hollered, "Happy birthday!"

"Lullabirds!" exclaimed Fordywinx. "How wonderful!"

Hubbub knelt down and opened the cage door. Every one of the Lullabirds left the cage and perched themselves in the branches of the big tree. As they began to sing, a feeling of comfort came to everyone listening.

"I don't have to count sheep anymore," said Fordywinx. "I'll count my blessings instead."

Listening to the soothing song of the Lullabirds, the old tree quietly dozed off.

After watching him fall asleep, Jubilee climbed the ladder into the tree fort. The rattle of the Jingle Jar sounded as she tiptoed back down. Jubilee had retrieved a Friendship Merit Pin from the jar. "This was for you too," she whispered to the sleeping tree, pinning it to one of his leaves. "For being such a good friend."

The children quietly made their way up into the tree fort. Revelly, in an amazing feat of self-restraint, resisted the urge to play his bugle with the song of the Lullabirds. After they showed Hubbub the fort, Gideon went to a storage chest and pulled out a small bundle of clothes.

"Welcome to the Tree Scouts, Hubbub," announced Gideon. "We want you to be our newest member."

Gideon handed him the brand new Tree Scout uniform. Hubbub was very pleased.

"Now you have to earn some Merit Pins!" exclaimed Revelly.

Hubbub loved being the newest member of the Tree Scouts. He couldn't wait to go on more adventures with his new friends. He looked forward to working with Gideon on new inventions.

After fond farewells, Hubbub headed home using the Bubblecraft. When the boat reached the island he made his way to the tree fort.

As suppertime approached the sun started it's slow descent. Hubbub lit the candle in his lantern for the walk home. He wondered to himself which Merit Pin he'd like to earn first. Then, as he started to leave, his lantern caused a shiny reflection that came from the jar on the table. Someone had put something in it! When he shook the jar it made a jingling sound.

Hubbub carefully took off the lid, reached in, and pulled out a Friendship Merit pin and a shiny Grabapple. He smiled to himself, realizing his new friends must have put them there. He grinned as he put the Merit Pin on his new Tree Scout uniform.

Hubbub sat for a while on the edge of his Tree Fort, thinking about his new friends and playing a Lullabird melody with his coat. "What a perfect gift for a good friend," he thought to himself. After descending the steps of thee tree fort he polished his Grabapple and took a large bite, munching it loudly all the way home.

The Silent Song
Of Wordishure

"I will praise the name of God with a song,
and will magnify him with thanksgiving."
Psalm 69:30

Little fingers jumped nimbly from key to key as music filled the foyer. The little red haired girl with the fast moving fingers practiced every day just after breakfast. Her name was Melody, aptly chosen because music about Jesus is what brought a big smile to her freckly face.

Her songs were quite popular in Newchime Village, where music played a large part in everyones life. Even the bellsmiths could ring Melody up for ideas, she always had specials notes just for them. Whenever Melody practiced new

ideas, she could hear neighbors singing or humming along as
they did laundry or just passed by. It reminded the girl of
how songs about God could bring joy or a repentant tear, and
a closeness to Jesus.

Melody could play almost any instrument and knew that
God had given her a special talent, so she made sure to use it
in a righteous way. Her old rosewood piano never sat quiet
long. The piano was handmade by her father, who was also a
bellsmith of Newchime.

As Melody practiced, a strong breeze picked up and blew
through the village, pushing open windows, doors, and even
caused a flap along the lines of their neighbors drying
laundry. She got up and closed the shutters, not noticing that
they didn't latch.

"I should get my kite out today, after rehearsal," Melody
thought. She loved flying kites, especially with her brother
Humphrey, who was the best kite flyer in all of Wordishure.
Melody knew he would be outside today. Their father, the
Bellsmith, had just given Humphrey a shiny blue kite for his
birthday.

When she returned to the piano for more practice, a new
song idea moved her spirit. Sitting at the piano, she felt the
Holy Spirit guiding her heart as she pressed the keys. Each
note sprung to life and their rich tones filled the room. "This
is perfect," she thought.

Melody got up from the piano and went into her bedroom,
pulled open her top dresser drawer, and looked inside.
Resting on top her clothes sat a beautiful leather bound

notebook that her mother had given her. She always encouraged her child's creativity. Melody picked up the notebook, hugged it, and carried it back to the piano.

After placing the notebook on top of the piano, she tapped the notes again and smiled. Grabbing her quill and ink, she began to jot down the notes the love of the Lord inspired. "This will be the special song for church on sunday" she thought.

Melody plunked keys, scribbled notes, hummed ideas, and jotted then tittled. The faster she wrote, the more inspired she became. She tucked her long hair behind each ear after she paused to re-ink her quill. Melody wanted to write something wonderful for Jesus, to share with everyone at Fellowship Church. As she was about to finish writing, the quill broke into two pieces as she pressed it against the paper.

"Mother has more quills in her thread basket," she mumbled out loud, more to herself than anyone in particular. Her mother loved to make quilts, so she usually kept plenty of quills around.

Melody looked around but could not find the basket. "It must be outside with mother," she remembered. Her mother often sat outside the window in her rocking chair listening to her daughter play. Melody opened the door and stepped outside to talk to her.

"We're all out of quills, Melody," said her mother when she saw Melody holding the broken quill. "We need to find more."

Just then, another breeze blew in through the open door

of the cottage! It was a strong gust and blew Melody's hair over her face. While brushing the hair away she heard the sound of rustling pages. Turning back toward the piano she saw the papers of her notebook being picked up by the wind. They were carried quickly out the window as the shutters blew open again.

"Oh no!" gasped Melody, running to the window. She could see all her writings being carried off in a handwritten whirlwind. Melody was heartbroken. She wanted to play something beautiful on Sunday, and now her notes were gone. Tears welled up in her soft green eyes as she watched the last bit of paper fly towards Gatherberry Hill, where she and Humphrey would fly their kites.

"Is something wrong Melody?" asked her mother, who had stepped inside and sat down with Melody at the piano, putting her arm around her.

"I'm sad mother," she said quietly. "I worked very hard on that song. I wanted so much to please Jesus on Sunday."

Her mother smiled, hugged her, and said, "Your heart is what pleases Jesus."

These wise words cheered Melody up a little bit. Melody's mother knelt down, brushed the tears away and said "I have a Cramberry pie in the stove. After it cools, would you like a piece?"

Melody loved gathering Cramberries for pies. They named them Cramberries because they were so good you couldn't cram them into your mouth fast enough! This made her feel much better. She smiled up at her mother and with a big nod said "Yes, ma'am!"

A short time later, the Cramberry pie sat cooling in the window next to Melody. She had returned to the piano and was trying to remember all the notes she had written. She tried not to be sad as she looked at the empty leather bound notebook lying in front of her.

Knock-knock-knock came a knock on the door. Melody got up to answer it. "Maybe it's the wind, returning my notes," she hoped.

"Who is it?" she asked.

"Is that Cramberry pie I smell?" came a familiar voice.

Melody recognized who it was and opened the door. It was her good friend Preston, the gopher. Preston loved Cramberries. As a matter of fact, he dug his home into Gatherberry Hill, just so he could eat all the Cramberries he wanted. "Would you like a piece?" Melody's mother asked as he stepped in.

"I sure would!" he cheerfully replied, following them to the table. "But they sure can be messy!"

"Make sure you use a napkin," Melody told the little brown gopher as she unfolded a napkin and laid it on her lap. "Cramberries are really juicy. Make sure they don't get on your clothes."

Preston, who was known for not liking to get dirty, wore spotlessly clean light blue overalls. Even when he dug his holes, he somehow managed to keep himself clean. He always dug slowly, carefully handling each piece of dirt like it was a spoonful of Cramberry pie. Melody was always amazed at how clean Preston was, because he was kind of clumsy too.

"I'm not worried about stains this time," he said while digging in his pocket. "I brought my own napkin."

As he tucked his napkin under his chin, Melody noticed that it wasn't a napkin at all.

"It's a page from my missing song!" she exclaimed, standing up from her chair. Melody ran over and hugged Preston, who nearly dropped his piece of Cramberry pie.

Preston untucked it and handed it to the smiling girl. "Where did you find this?" she asked.

"I found it lying on the ground near one of my tunnels. Up on Gatherberry Hill," the gopher responded. "Maybe there's

more up there."

After finishing her snack, Melody got her mother's permission to search for her missing song. "Be home for devotions," advised her mom as Melody went to the piano.

"I will ma'am," she responded, picking up her leather bound notebook case. Melody and Preston waved goodbye and left the cottage, heading toward the base of the beautiful green hill that sat in the distance.

Walking over the grassy field that led up the hill, Preston grew short of breath. "Too much Cramberry pie!" he panted while rubbing his belly. "Just let me catch my breath."

Preston spotted an old tree stump nearly hidden in some tall grass and walked over to it. He made sure to brush it off nicely before sitting down.

"Please don't sit on my house!" came a muffled voice from inside the stump.

As soon as he heard the voice, Preston leaped from the stump and fell headfirst into a nearby pile of leaves.

"My clean clothes!" fretted Preston, quickly standing back up. "Are there any stains on them?!"

A small yellow bird with a small feather sticking up on his head emerged from a hole inside the stump. "I didn't mean to scare you," it chirped. "But I thought you were going to crush me!"

Melody walked over to the stump and knelt down to talk to the jittery bird. "I'm Melody," she said, "and this is my friend Preston. He didn't mean any harm. We're on our way to Gatherberry Hill to find the missing pages of my song."

"Like these?" the little bird warbled, pointing to his hidden nest in the stump.

When Melody looked down, she could see two of the missing pages lying in the bird's nest. "I found them up on the hill, he noted, "I thought the music was beautiful. Not only do the pages keep my nest warm, reading them warms my heart as I tried to sing the tune."

"We sure would like them back, Mr. Bird," said Preston, picking the leaves from his overalls.

"My name is Walker," chirped the happy, little bird.

"That's a strange name for a bird," said Melody while gathering her pages from the nest.

"I got that name because I'm scared of heights," Walker explained. "I prefer to walk safely on the ground."

"We're still missing two pages, Preston," noted Melody, placing the newly found pages into her notebook.

"Let's keep moving up," said Preston, brushing off the last of the leaves.

"Can I come along?" asked Walker. "Maybe I can help you complete your journey."

"Okay," said Preston. "I hope your tiny legs can keep up."

As they traveled closer to the top of the hill, they could hear music coming from a nearby circle of trees. It was the beautiful sound of harps playing. "That's my song they're playing!" exclaimed Melody before racing off towards the music.

"Wait for me!" chirped Walker.

Reaching the clearing in the trees she could see three little birds, sitting on a tree branch, playing the smallest harps she had ever seen. "Those are Strummingbirds!" observed Walker.

Below the Strummingbirds was a porcupine that lay sound asleep on the ground. And there, sticking to some quills on his back, was a page of the music Melody had written.

"There's one of your pages!" commented Preston as he stepped forward and tripped, landing in a Squishberry bush. "Oh no!" he exclaimed.

The Strummingbirds stopped playing when they heard Preston fall over. "Are you okay?" they chuckled.

"Mmm hmmm," mumbled Preston, as he tasted the squishberries that were smushed on his overalls.

"Why did you stop playing?" yawned the porcupine as he stood up and stretched. "I was having such a good nap."

"My name's Melody," said the little girl, walking up to the porcupine. "And a page of my song is stuck to your back."

"I was wondering why these Strummingbirds kept following me around," he replied while trying to see behind his back.

"My name is Quilliam. I'd shake your hand but, well, you know..." he said flicking one of the quills on his paw.

Walker ran over and plucked the page off the back of the porcupine with his beak. "Where do you think you sat on this?" asked Melody.

"I was watching this boy fly a kite on top of Gatherberry Hill. He got the kite so high up in the air, it bumped into a cloud!" recalled Quilliam.

"That's way too high!" commented Walker after he set the

page into Melody's hand.

"I came down here to eat some lunch," said Quilliam. "That's when these Strummingbirds appeared and started playing this beautiful song. It relaxed me so much I decided to take a quick nap."

"That boy sounds like my brother Humphrey," said Melody. "He took his new kite out this morning. Can you show us where he's at?"

Smiling, Quilliam pointed into the air.

Everyone looked up at the sky. And there, flying next to a big fluffy cloud with a dent in it, soared a shiny blue kite. "Just follow the string down," said Quilliam.

"Can we come too?" the Strummingbirds sang in unison. "We'd like to learn more of the song."

Melody agreed and everyone went up the hill. Upon reaching the top they found Humphrey lying in the grass with his legs crossed. He was holding the kite with a string he had wrapped around his big toe. "Hi Sis," greeted Humphrey. "What are you doing up here? I thought you were going to practice the piano today."

"I did, but I had a song idea. My writing quill broke before I could finish writing the last note," explained Melody. "Then a gust of wind arose, and blew the song's pages out of the window."

"My heart was broken until my friend Preston knocked on the door," she beamed while placing a hand on his shoulder. "He had found what I had been missing! Then we started the journey upwards. We've found all the pages except one. It's

the page that needed to
be finished."

"Is that your page?"
asked Humphrey,
pointing up to his kite.
When they looked up,
they could see the last,
unfinished page of
Melody's song was
caught inside it.

"There it is!"
exclaimed Preston,
gazing up in the sky. "It must have got caught in the kite as it
was flying around."

Preston backed up a few steps for a better look and
bumped into Quilliam. "Ouch!" he yelled, jumping from
being poked by a quill.

As the gopher leaping forward, he tripped over the string
that was holding the kite aloft. They all gasped as the string
snapped and the kite went soaring upward.

"Oh no!" cried Melody. "The song will be lost forever!"

"No it won't," chirped Walker, racing into the air.
Everyone stood in awe at Walker's new found bravery.
Melody decided to lead them in a prayer for Walker's safety,
who now faced his fear of flying to help his new friends.

Walker flew higher and higher into the sky until he
became worried and filled with doubt. Suddenly, he felt
himself begin to fall. Looking down, he could see that all his

friends were praying for him. Realizing that God answers prayer, it lifted his spirit upward, and he felt renewed. Walker went up so high he could see all over the land of Wordishure. He was amazed at the beauty of God's handiwork. He felt ashamed that he had let his fears kept him from flying and being what God had made him to be. But he was encouraged by the thought that he was created special, and he could now fly higher than he ever thought possible. Who knew that finding a new song could change his life so much. "Thank you Lord!" he chirped before his beak latched onto the kite.

The children below let out a cheer as the little bird triumphantly guided the kite back down to the ground. They all praised God and congratulated Walker on his personal victory.

"I almost lost my best kite," said Humphrey, letting out a sigh of relief.

He pulled Melody's page from the kite and handed it to her.

"Can we hear the song now?" asked Preston, rubbing his sore spot from the quill poke.

Melody suddenly remembered that the song was unfinished. "I forgot that I couldn't finish it because my writing quill broke."

"I can help now, too!" declared Quilliam. He quickly plucked a quill from his shoulder and handed it to Melody. "Now I can be a part of finishing your song."

They all laughed and played on the hill for a while before heading back home. Melody had invited everyone to hear her play the song at Fellowship Church on Sunday. They were excited and couldn't wait to hear it. She even invited the Strummingbirds to come and rehearse with her.

When Melody and Humphrey arrived back in time for devotions, she told their mother and father about her exciting day. They were relieved that the children were home on-time and that Melody had found her song. After supper, Melody sat back down at the piano and played the song again. Only this time, she finished writing the notes with the quill that the Quilliam had given her. She couldn't wait to play it for all her new friends and the people at Fellowship church.

When Sunday came, music could be heard all around the floating church as it sailed along Waterdove Lake during the service. Preston, wearing new overalls, sat next to Walker, who flew in and perched in a windowsill. Quilliam sat there too, but not too close. Humphrey, with neatly combed hair and a tie made from kite string, sat with Melody's parents in the front row.

The Strummingbirds played along on their harps as Melody finally got to play her special song. As she played she realized that the special song was even better now, because it had the chance to be touched by so many others. No one would have gotten to hear it if it wasn't for the friends that God had brought into her life.

When the song ended, she left the piano and sat down with her parents. The Pastor walked up to the platform and opened God's Word. After he finished preaching and was giving an invitation for people to come to the altar, Melody got up and went back to the piano.

As she softly played, many of the people came to the altar to ask forgiveness or pray. That's when Melody realized the real music wasn't coming from her piano; it came from the chords that played in people's hearts. The chords were struck when people came forward to rest their burdens on Jesus.

Melody stopped playing, walked up to the altar, and knelt down. That's when she remembered her mother's wise words, "Your heart is what pleases Jesus." She thanked the Lord for everything He had done, realizing that prayer was the real song that God wanted to hear. Although not a sound could be heard throughout Fellowship Church, the most beautiful song that couldn't be heard was playing in each person's heart. It was the silent song, prayer.

The Church Mice
Of Wordishure

"And he shall send his angels with a great sound of a trumpet,
and they shall gather together his elect from the four winds,
from one end of heaven to the other."
Matthew 24:31

Early one Sunday morning, as Fellowship Church sat docked on Waterdove Lake, a small light flickered from a hole above the church piano. Inside the hole lived three little church mice, two of which, were sound asleep.

Colby, the oldest brother, snored loudly and licked his lips. He was dreaming about this upcoming morning's Squishberry pancakes. Topped, of course, with lots of four-leaf clover honey. Pepper, his younger sister, slept soundly with her sleeping cap pulled down over her ears to block out

Colby's loud snoring. Jack, the youngest of the three mice, sat on his bed reading his Bible by candlelight. He loved to read God's Word, especially about all the heroes of the faith whose trust in God got them through the most challenging of situations. Jack had hardly slept a wink. He was too excited about being in the church play this morning.

Colby, Pepper, and Jack were cast to play the parts of the three lions in "Daniel in the Lions Den". They practiced being lions for weeks. Jack was so anxious, that he wore his lion costume to bed! While rubbing his eyes, he let out a quick yawn.

"Creeeaaakk," came a noise. "That's odd," Jack thought. "I've squeaked, but never creaked."

He opened his mouth again. "Creeaakkkk," he quickly closed it again. Jack put his hand over his mouth and peered over at his sleeping siblings. "Creeaaakk," came the noise again. "If I'm not creaking," he wondered, "what's making that sound?"

Then came other noises: a groan, a pop, and then a loud KABONG that shook the entire ship! It sounded like something big had crashed above him on the upper deck. "The church bell!" exclaimed Jack, recognizing the sound of the Fellowship Church bell.

"What was that?" grumbled Colby, sitting upright before climbing out of his bed. When Colby stood up, bits of hay fell out onto the floor. He rushed over to Jack, passing Pepper, who was still asleep with her ears covered.

"Let's go see what happened," Jack told Colby, leading

him by his pajama sleeve. They raced out of the hole onto the piano and climbed down its side. Then they leaped onto the wooden staircase leading to the upper deck. That's when they attempted to tiptoe over the squeaky board they knew was halfway up the stairs. "Squeak!" came the sound from the board as Jack stepped on it. "Shh," Colby warned as he gently set his toe down. "Squeak!" came the sound again. Colby winced then shrugged his shoulders at Jack. The two brothers could have been a little more careful, but everyone knows how hard it is for a mouse not to squeak.

Once at the top, they saw the church bell lying on the deck with a big crack running up its side. Lying beside it was the rope that used to hold it in place.

"Maybe it's just a scratch," Colby remarked hopefully, walking up to touch the bell where it was cracked.

"Then its the biggest scratch ever!" answered Jack from inside the bell, peering out at Colby through the crack. "How will people know when it's time to come to church? Everyone's going to miss the church play!"

"It looks like somebody nibbled off bits of the rope," came a familiar voice from behind the bell.

Startled, Colby and Jack nearly fell over. Their friend Honx the goose waddled out into view. "You gave us a good scare, Honx," stammered Colby.

"Yes," agreed Jack, straightening out the fur on his lion costume. "I'm supposed to be the scary one today."

"Sorry to frighten you. I was delivering this morning's Squishberries from Trusthymn Village when I heard the kabong, so I decided to investigate. I found this rope behind the bell."

As the two brothers approached Honx, they could see that the rope had been nibbled on.

"Uh oh," commented Colby as he examined the rope. "I think this may be my fault."

"That isn't hay in your bed, is it?" Jack asked Colby while plucking a bit of rope strand from his brother's pajamas.

Colby rubbed his nose and said, "I get hay fever. Besides, this rope is really soft." He rubbed the rope strand on his cheek and pretended to purr like a cat. "I can purr, I'm supposed to be a lion today," shrugged the little brown mouse.

"But lions don't chew on ropes," came a voice from behind them.

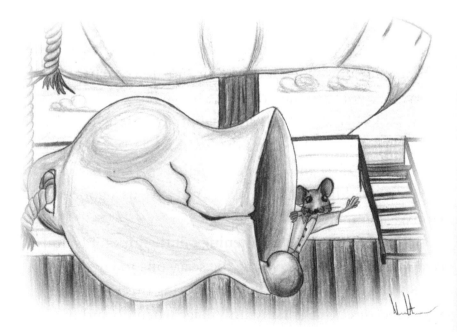

It was Pepper, glaring at them with her arms crossed. She was up early and already wearing her favorite green dress with yellow polka dots, for Sunday services. "And they certainly don't snore!"

"We thought you were still asleep," said Jack.

"The squeaky board woke me up," replied Pepper as she examined the rope. "I can sleep through loud crashes and even Colby's snoring, but I can't let a squeak go by without checking on you two."

"Why would you nibble on the same part of the rope?" Jack asked Colby.

"It's the only part I could reach," confessed his older brother.

"If we don't fix the bell, my friend Edward and his grandma won't know when to be here to make squishberry pancakes!" worried Honx, patting his belly.

"Maybe the Tree Scouts can help fix the bell!" suggested Jack. He knew that the Tree Scouts loved to help others. "We need to go to Springwater Lake and find Gideon the inventor. I bet he can fix this."

"But Springwater Lake is quite a distance from here," noted Pepper.

"I can fly you there," honked Honx. "It sounds like an adventure!"

"I hope your friend can help," said the pastor of Fellowship Church, as he walked up to examine the crack in the bell.

Colby hung his head and apologized, "I'm sorry Pastor. I

promise never to do it again."

The Pastor knelt down, picked Colby up in his hand and said, "Everyone makes mistakes, Colby, and it is important to apologize," then he placed his finger over Colby's heart. "But this bell will never ring unless someone takes time to fix it."

"I'll say!" agreed Honx, wiping his wing across a Squishberry stain on his feathers.

The Pastor set Colby back down with the others. "I must go finish my sermon, but first let's pray for your journey. You'll need to reach as many people as you can before it's too late."

The three mice all looked at each other. Jack in his lion costume, Pepper in her fancy dress, and Colby still wearing his pajamas. "We're ready," said Jack as they prayed with Pastor and asked God to be with them. Colby knew in his heart that he had done wrong, and wanted to make things right with the Lord. Trying to fix a mistake without God is a bigger mistake, he thought.

"Be careful with those claws," joked Honx as Jack and the mice climbed onto his back. "And hang on!"

The three mice each held on tight as Honx lowered his head, spread out his wings and waddled to the edge of the deck where he leaped into the air. They flew high above Waterdove Lake, where the mice could see many of the multi-colored trees that decorated the beautiful land of Wordishure. As Honx glided over Trusthymn Village, they approached Lil' Valley pond, where they landed to say hello to Edward and Sam Phibian, who were practicing skipping stones.

"Hello mices," greeted Edward as he crouched down by the goose.

The mice explained their situation to the boy and the frog. "We'll tell everyone we know to come to church," agreed Sam.

"Can we come with you to find Gideon," Edward asked eagerly.

"I don't think I can carry all of you, Edward. You're a lot bigger than the mice!" chuckled Honx.

"That's okay," laughed Edward. "We need to get to Tumbledown Hill and invite some special friends."

"And tumble down the hill!" added Sam.

"We'll see you at church," hollered Jack as Honx took to the sky once more.

"See you soon, mices!" replied Edward.

Traveling onward, they passed over Squintville, Uppatree Forest, and then Rickety Bridge. They observed the Bridge Mizer napping quietly next to his beloved bridge. He was wearing a wide-brimmed hat to keep himself shaded.

"I used to eat his hats," came a voice from above.

As Honx and the three mice looked up they could see a large green dragon flying over them. "Now I like candy," she noted.

"Hello Brimnibble," greeted Pepper, smiling at the mighty dragon. "We're on a quest to find Gideon and the Tree Scouts. The church bell is broken so nobody will know when it's time to come to church."

"That sounds like fun," said Brimnibble. "Is there any way I can help?" she asked.

"Help us to spread the word. If everyone listens, we'll all be together praising God," hollered Colby up to the dragon.

"My hats off to you, church mice." said Brimnibble. "I'll fly to the castle right now."

Then Brimnibble flew off toward Wordishure Castle to inform the King, Queen and their three daughters. The mice were confident that Princesses Irelynd, Tara, and Ashtyn would bring everyone they knew to church on time. And besides, whoever heard of a late princess?

"There's Ontoppa Hill!" pointed Jack as they approached the largest hill in all of Wordishure.

"The Humblebees are collecting honey," noticed Pepper, watching them flying around their hive with tiny buckets of honey. Since joining the church, the bee's brought honey every Sunday morning for everyone to put on their Squishberry pancakes. Filmore the cat was down by the bee's hive, helping to make sure not one drop of honey went to waste.

Bix, the bee, recognized the mice from church and flew up and gave them each a bit of honeycomb. "I thought lions didn't eat honey," joked Bix, handing one to Jack.

"I'm not really a lion, Mr. Bix," replied Jack while licking his lips. "But I do have a sweet lions' tooth!"

The mice told Bix about the broken bell, and that they hoped to have it fixed. "I'll tell Filmore and the other bees," Bix offered before buzzing back down to the hive. Filmore waved hello to them as they flew overhead. The mice giggled when they noticed all the honey stains around his big grin.

Traveling farther along, the mice ate their honeycomb and

sang '*I'll Fly Away*'. "It sure is great to soar above the clouds," said Pepper to Honx as she closed her eyes, feeling the breeze on her face.

"It sure is," came the voice of Walker the Warbler. "I didn't realize there was an angel up here too," he chirped, making Pepper blush.

The three mice each said hello to Walker as Honx glided over next to him.

"What are you doing here?" asked the little yellow bird. "Aren't you supposed to be in the Lion's Den today?"

"The church bell is cracked and won't make a sound," answered Colby. "We're on our way to see Gideon at his Tree Fort. We're hoping he can invent something to take its place until it's fixed."

"Melody's father can fix the bell," Walker informed them. "He's the Bellsmith in Newchime Village."

The mice let out a sigh of relief; they all knew Melody and her family from church. Melody would play the piano as they sang special songs. "Let's find him!" exclaimed Colby, "What a blessing!"

"It will take time to fix the bell," Pepper reminded Colby, "We still need to find Gideon."

"He'll come up with something," said Jack, patting his brother on the back. "He's a great inventor!"

Walker let them know that he would find Melody's father and flew toward Newchime Village. They were all grateful they had friends in high places! A short time later, Honx and the mice had arrived at Springwater Lake.

"There's the tree fort," noticed Honx as he gently glided down. The goose landed on the ground directly in front of the Sleeping Willow tree that held Gideon's tree fort.

"Hello everyone," greeted the Sleeping Willow. "Are you looking for Gideon?"

"We sure are, Fordywinx," answered Honx.

"Are these the mighty lions in the church play?" asked the big tree.

"Roar!" growled Jack, raising his claws into the air.

"My, my, that was a mighty roar!" laughed the tree. "I think you may have frightened the sheep in Shepard's Field!"

A few sheep in the nearby field looked up from their grazing. "I hope I didn't scare them too much," worried Jack.

"I'm sure they'll recover," winked Fordywinx. "If you're looking for Gideon, he held a campout for the new Tree Scouts at Hubbub's tree fort. It's over on Bearfruit Island," he added. "One of my Lullabirds can show you the way."

"Thank you so much, Mr. Tree," said Colby. "We have to get everyone to the church on time!"

"Speaking of time," smiled Fordywinx, "You woke me just in time for my nap. Come back and visit anytime."

As Fordywinx finished his sentence the Lullabirds started to sing a beautiful song that lulled the big tree back to sleep. As the other birds sang, one flew from a branch and beckoned the mice to follow. Honx and his passengers took to the air and flew toward Bearfruit Island. On the way, Pepper spotted an unusually large tree along the shore.

"Look!" said Pepper. "That's a Grabapple Tree!"

As they flew closer, they spotted two animals with springs on their feet bouncing around and waving for them to land. It was Dilly and Dally, the two Woodashoodas who loved Grabapples. After landing and explaining their situation, the mice invited them to church and they both agreed. "The Bible teaches us to answer whenever the Lord calls," said Dilly.

"No more would've should've when it comes to loving God," noted Dally. "Today is the day!"

The three mice, Honx, and the Lullabird all enjoyed a Grabapple before leaving for Bearfruit Island. "Say hello to Hubbub for us," the Woodashoodas called out. "Tell him to save us a seat at church!"

As the mice flew closer to the island, they could see everything on it. The tree fort, a lakeside house, and even a small boat docked along the shore.

After making sure they could reach the tree fort, the Lullabird waved goodbye and flew off to join the rest of his flock. The mice waved back as Honx slowly glided downward, landing at the bottom step that lead up to Hubbubs tree fort. The three mice jumped down off Honx and started to climb the steps. "Shhh," shushed Pepper, raising a finger to her lips. "It's still early, they may still be asleep."

"I'll be quiet as a church mouse," Colby reassured Pepper, jumping to the first step.

"Squeak!" The stair squeaked loudly. "Oh no," Colby said slapping his paw on his forehead. "Another squeaky stair!"

"Hello," came a voice from the top of the stairs. It was Hubbub the Tree Scout, "What are you church mice doing here? Shouldn't you be getting ready for the play?"

"The church bell is broken," Pepper told Hubbub. "We came to see if the Tree Scouts could help find a way to alert all the people of Wordishure that it's time for church."

Hubbub beckoned them to come up into the tree fort. "Watch the squeaky step," he joked.

Upon entering the tree fort, all the Tree Scouts looked up at them from Hubbubs invention table. Not only was Gideon there, but also Micah and Jonah, who had recently joined the Tree Scouts. "Guess what we're doing!" exclaimed Jonah with a big smile. "We're building a new tree fort in the big shade tree by Oldwood Creek."

"We didn't miss church today," worried Micah, seeing Jack in his lion costume. "Because we haven't heard the church bell."

Pepper quickly explained what happened and how they needed everyone's help. Micah was relieved that he didn't miss church and was eager to help the church mice.

Gideon and Hubbub paced back and forth for a few moments trying to think of an invention that would let people know when church began. "I think I can help!" declared Micah as he ran to get his backpack. He pulled out an old tattered scroll and spread it out across the table. "This was in my Grandpa's old wooden chest. My mother keeps it in the attic," he explained.

It was a rough drawing of the largest kite any of them had ever seen. "Grandpa used to take me kite flying," remembered Micah fondly. "This was going to be his greatest invention!"

"It looks huge!"
commented Colby.
Hubbub picked up the
three mice and set them
on the table.

"Let's go build it!" said
Jonah, grabbing at the
drawing. "I love kites!"

Gideon stopped him and said, "Hold on Jonah, a Tree
Scout has to be patient. Besides, I have a few modifications
I'd like to make to this drawing."

"Me too," said Hubbub. "Let me show you..."

Hubbub grabbed a nearby quill, dipped it in some ink and
began to draw. Then Gideon made his notes when Hubbub
finished. Once they were done, everyone stood around the
drawing and smiled in approval.

"It's even better now!" exclaimed Colby.

"And tasty too," Jack said, nibbling the edge of the drawing.

"How can we build this?" asked Jonah.

"It will take all of our friends and plenty of bravery. But
most of all, we need to trust the Lord," Gideon answered.

Once Gideon explained what the plan was, they all
nodded in agreement. They were glad that God made
everyone unique and special. They all said a prayer of thanks
that even little church mice could make a difference for so
many others.

A short time later, Honx was back in the air with the mice.
Gideon had told them to find Bigby the Giant, and to find

the strongest Oakypine wood available. The top branches of Oakypines are sturdy, almost as light as a Cactickle feather, and perfect for flying an extra large kite. Honx flew as fast as he could toward Meadowvalley Glenn, hoping to find the friendly giant right away.

"This is farther than I thought," honked Honx wearily. "I need a short rest."

He spotted a large stone in the woods below him and landed on it. The mice noticed "Walkdown Trail" was carved into the surface of the stone.

"Walkdown Trail leads to Meadowvalley Glenn," Pepper told Honx. "Bigby must be close by."

"I'm afraid not," came a voice from behind a tree branch that was hanging over a corner of the stone.

Colby and Pepper pulled Honx's feathers up over their faces to hide while Jack stood up and raised his lion claws. "Who said that?" he growled.

Turner, the chameleon, emerged from behind the branch. He had been difficult to see at first because he was wearing his camouflage. "Phew," Honx said relaxing. "We didn't see you there."

"I'm practicing for Seek the Lost," stated Turner. "Bigby, Filmore, and I love playing that game after church."

"We're seeking Bigby right now!" explained Colby. "Maybe you can help us!"

Pepper quickly explained their situation and why it was so important that they find Bigby. Turner knew exactly where Bigby was and promised to guide them there. "He takes a swim every morning at Bigwater Falls. I'll take you there right now!" said Turner, climbing onto Honx's back.

"I hope my back can handle this," worried Honx as he gathered his strength on the rock. As the goose leaped up into the air, Turner let out a whoop!

As they came to the bustling village of Bigwater Falls, named after the big waterfall nearby, they spotted Bigby playing by the water with a couple of children. Bigby was dressed up in robes as God's prophet, Daniel. He wore a big beard made from straw that the two children were collecting for him.

"Hello, Lions!" he waved as Honx and the church mice landed in front of him. "Did Turner bring you here to help me rehearse? I was just practicing my lines with my friends Philip and Abby.

"We're good at repeating things," stated Abby, while giving each of their visitors a small piece of candy.

"Don't fill up on candy," warned Philip, "we're having Squishberry pancakes at church!"

After the mice explained their situation, along with Gideon and Hubbubs' plan, Bigby told them he knew where to locate the best Oakypine tree. With Turner on his shoulder, he led them through the woods to the tallest Oakypine in the forest.

Bigby spotted the perfect branches way up at the top. "Even I can't reach those," said Bigby.

Philip tugged at Bigby's robe and said, "Let me climb up, I'm the best tree climber in all of Wordishure!"

Abby nodded in agreement. So Bigby picked Philip up and put him high up into the Oakypine branches. Philip climbed higher and higher until he was at the tippy-top. He plucked off the branches and tossed them down to Bigby. The mice let out a cheer. Everyone congratulated Bigby for being so uplifting, and Philip for reaching for the top.

"We've got to get these branches back to Fellowship Church," explained Pepper. "The others are waiting for us."

Bigby tucked the branches into his robe and said, "You fly there as fast as you can. I can run the whole way. I know which path to follow."

While Philip and Abby headed home to let their parents know that it was time to leave for church, Honx and the church mice started their flight towards Waterdove Lake. They watched Bigby running below them as they flew. The loud thump, thump, thump from Bigby's feet could be heard all around. Turner, the chameleon, was hanging on Bigby's shoulder, giggling loudly and enjoying the ride.

As the time for church approached the mice knew they had to hurry. If their prayers were going to be answered, they knew they had to do their part as well.

"Here we are!" proclaimed Honx, spotting Gideon waving to them from the top deck of Fellowship Church. Standing with Gideon and tooting his horn with delight was Revelly the squirrel and his sister Jubilee. As they landed, Bigby emerged from the trail and headed to the dock. He stepped onto the big boat and set the Oakypine branches down in front of Gideon, who immediately laid out Jubilee's napping blanket and set the sticks on top of it.

"Are you sure that's where they go?" Revelly asked Gideon.

"The sticks must be laid out in a cross, Revelly," answered the boy. "It gives the kite proper support. Without the cross everything would fall apart."

"Now we need to sew the sticks onto the blanket," explained Gideon. "I hope Hubbub was able to find our other friends."

Then, from off in the distance, a familiar sound drew closer. "Look!" Jubilee called out, "It's Hubbub with the Bubblecraft!"

Jubilee was right. Hubbub, wearing his Coat of Many Noises, came into sight as he steered the Bubblecraft towards them. But he wasn't alone. Also on the bubble-powered boat were Melody, Humphrey, Quilliam the porcupine, and Preston the gopher. The three Strummingbirds flew over their heads, playing in tune with Hubbub's musical coat. When they arrived at the boat, Bigby reached down and lifted each one of them from the Bubblecraft and onto the deck. "Ouch!" exclaimed Bigby, as he set Quilliam down.

"Sorry!" apologized Quilliam. "I always dress sharp for church."

"I'll say," replied Bigby, putting his finger in his mouth.

Gideon asked Quilliam if he could use one of his quills to sew the kite together.

"I'd love to help," responded Quilliam, plucking a quill and handing it to Gideon.

"Does anyone know how to sew?" said Colby as he and his

siblings climbed down from Honx's back.

"I help my mom sew all the time," claimed Melody, kneeling down next to the kite. "But we'll need some string."

Melody's brother Humphrey knelt down by his sister and loosened his necktie made from kite string. "This should help," he said, handing it to her.

"It's just the right amount," smiled the girl.

Melody took the string and the quill and quickly began sewing the kite together. When she finished, she looked up at Gideon and said, "What about a tail? A kite cannot fly without a tail."

Just then, a large shadow passed over all the figures standing on the deck of the ship. "Maybe we can help," came a voice from above them. It was Cahoots the owl, carrying a large sock basket. Micah, Jonah, and Argyle the sock weasel, were waving to them from inside.

"You got here fast!" said Jack as Cahoots lowered the basket to let the passengers climb out.

"The Chatterbugs heard through the vine that we were coming," replied Micah, referring to the Chatterbugs who were sitting on Argyle's furry white shoulder.

"He who has ears, let him hear..." Tsk Tsk, the Chatterbug, said, quoting Scripture.

"And those with furry ears, as well," laughed Tut Tut, tapping his walking stick on Argyle's ear.

"Good news travels fast," observed Tsk Tsk, noticing Edward and Sam Phibian as they hopped aboard the ship.

"We brought our friends with us!" proclaimed Edward.

Suddenly, a swarm of fireflies, led by Taylite and Liddlelite flew onto the deck and circled them. Their tails all lit up when they saw the giant kite, "It needs a tail," declared Liddlelite.

"Here's the tail!" said Argyle the sock weasel, handing Melody the kite's tail that he had made from socks. "They've been washed too," noted the sock weasel.

Melody sewed the tail onto the end of the large kite. "It's ready to fly," she proclaimed.

Everyone let out a cheer and praised God that everything had come together so far.

The church mice clapped loudly with Jubilee as Bigby picked up the kite and let Revelly climb onto it. "I hope this plan works," he said nervously, "because I wasn't born a flying squirrel!"

Revelly clutched his bugle tightly as the giant tossed the kite high into the air. Everyone gasped as the kite struggled to remain aloft. That's when Cahoots, the owl, flew in, grabbed the kite, and flew it back up into the air. The wind blew much stronger this high and took the kite upward even farther. "I can't fly any higher," panted Cahoots before releasing the kite. Revelly held on tight as the kite flew up near a fluffy white cloud.

Revelly relaxed a bit when he saw that Humphrey, the best kite flyer in all of Wordishure was holding the string. "Send up the fireflies!" Revelly shouted to the crowd below.

Gideon walked over to his jar of collected bubbles and opened the lid. As the bubbles rose into the air, Taylite,

Liddlelite, and all the other fireflies each jumped inside them. When the bubbles reached Revelly and the kite, Hubbub signaled for the squirrel to sound the music.

Revelly, always eager to play, licked his lips, and took a deep breath. Then he trumped the bugle louder than he ever had before. At the sound of the horn all the fireflies lit up their tails inside the bubbles, which magnified their lights in every direction. Everyone on the deck below stood in awe at the beauty of the large red kite being illuminated in the morning sky. Miniature rainbows glimmered all over the land of Wordishure. It reminded them of the promise God made to Noah.

Cheers from the deck below could be heard as the bugle sounded out the most beautiful morning song that ever welcomed anyone to church. From all around, the residents of Wordishure stepped out of their homes and watched. With uplifted spirits, people started their way toward Fellowship Church, anxious to hear God's Word.

People started boarding the ship as Revelly played louder and stronger. That's when the church mice climbed onto the backs of the three Strumming birds, who gracefully flew them upward through the rainbow-like maze of bubbles surrounding the kite. "Thank you, Revelly!" shouted each of the church mice, "It's okay to come down now."

Revelly let out one last "Toot!" and slid down the kite string.

After the people boarded the ship they all met in the giant galley for a hearty breakfast of squishberry pancakes. Edward, his grandmother, and Sam Phibian served the pancakes from a wobbly pancake wagon. Everyone covered their pancakes with lots of the four-leaf clover honey that the Humblebees brought.

After breakfast, everyone congregated inside Fellowship Church's main hall to hear God's Word and to praise God in

song. Bigby, standing much taller than the rest, shouted "Amen!" from the back as the songs moved his giant heart.

Melody played the hymn, "Only Trust Him", while Princess Irelynd sang. After she finished singing, the Pastor gave a special thanks to the church mice, and everyone else who was involved in bringing the people of Wordishure together. The Pastor preached a message about the bell, and how it was a picture of their hearts. Both could be broken and left in disrepair, but they could also be fixed, and ring joyfully for all to hear!

Later, after the church service, everyone stayed to watch the church play, "Daniel in the Lions Den." Bigby, playing Daniel, was very courageous. He was willing to face the ferocious church mice dressed up as lions, just so he could obey God. The audience all laughed when Bigby knelt down just so he could hear the tiny roars of church mice.

When the play was over, they all received a standing ovation. As they took their bows, the Pastor thanked all the people for coming and reminded the people of Wordishure about putting their trust in the Lord, even if they faced frightening lions, like Colby, Pepper, and Jack.

Everyone in the church held their Bibles in the air and shouted, "Amen!"

The service finished with a song and a loud blast from Revelly's bugle. Each person went home with a thankful spirit, lifted heart, and a renewed confidence in the authority of God's Word, because in the Land of Wordishure, His Word is Sure.

If you enjoyed this book and would like to help this children's ministry, please remember it in your prayers. You can also, go to Amazon.com and write a review or recommend it to your friends on Goodreads.com. This will help the Wordishure series reach more people.

Mick & Erica McArt

About the Author

Mick McArt was raised in Tawas, Michigan and was a young man when he gave his heart to the Lord. After high school he became an assembler in an automotive plant. Inspired to pursue more, he applied for college at 22 years old. He delivered pizza to help pay his way through college. After graduating, he started a professional career in multimedia design at a large manufacturing facility, where he is currently employed.

Mick sees his imagination as a gift from God and hopes to use it to be a blessing to others. With encouragement from his wife, pastor, and friends, Mick began work on this book.

He currently attends Faith Baptist Church, in Saginaw, Michigan. There he met and married his wife Erica. They currently live in Saginaw with their newborn son Micah.

Mick earned a Bachelor of Fine Arts degree from Central Michigan University and a Masters degree from Saginaw Valley State University.

Mick spends his spare time being creative and working on many projects. This book is the fruit of that God-given talent.

Also available from the Wordishure Series:
Tales of Wordishure: Book II
The Silent Knight of Wordishure Book
Songs of Wordishure CD
Coming soon: Tales of Wordishure: Book III

Other books available through
Mick Art Productions Publishing:
Beacons of Light by Mick McArt
Casey Brand New by Janis Lord
Redeemed by Charles C. Smith
Night of Destiny - A Survivor's Story by Kelly Ann Reed
The Empty Birdfeeder by Theresa Wyatt

MICK ART
PRODUCTIONS LLC
PUBLISHING
www.mickartproductions.com

CPSIA information can be obtained at www.ICGtesting.com
Printed in the USA
BVOW10s1740291113

337600BV00005B/10/P